THE GUEST OF QUESNAY

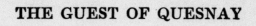

Several pairs of brighter eyes followed my companion

THE GUEST OF QUESNAY

BY

BOOTH TARKINGTON

ILLUSTRATED

NEW YORK
CHARLES SCRIBNER'S SONS
1916

TO
OVID BUTLER JAMESON

LIST OF ILLUSTRATIONS

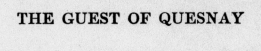

THE GUEST OF QUESNAY

CHAPTER I

THERE are old Parisians who will tell you pompously that the boulevards, like the political cafés, have ceased to exist, but this means only that the boulevards no longer gossip of Louis Napoleon, the Return of the Bourbons, or of General Boulanger, for these highways are always too busily stirring with present movements not to be forgetful of their yesterdays. In the shade of the buildings and awnings, the loungers, the lookers-on in Paris, the audience of the boulevard, sit at little tables, sipping coffee from long glasses, drinking absinthe or bright-coloured *sirops*, and gazing over the heads of throngs afoot at others borne along through the sunshine of the street in carriages, in cabs, in glittering automobiles, or high on the tops of omnibuses.

From all the continents the multitudes come to join in that procession: Americans, tagged with race-cards and intending hilarious disturbances; puzzled Americans, worn with guide-book plodding;

Chinese princes in silk; queer Antillean dandies of
swarthy origin and fortune; ruddy English, thinking of nothing; pallid English, with upper teeth
bared and eyes hungrily searching for sign-boards
of tea-rooms; over-Europeanised Japanese, unpleas-
antly immaculate; burnoosed sheiks from the desert,
and red-fezzed Semitic peddlers; Italian nobles in
English tweeds; Soudanese negroes swaggering in
frock coats; slim Spaniards, squat Turks, travellers,
idlers, exiles, fugitives, sportsmen—all the tribes
and kinds of men are tributary here to the Parisian
stream which, on a fair day in spring, already over-
flows the banks with its own much-mingled waters.
Soberly clad burgesses, bearded, amiable, and in no
fatal hurry; well-kept men of the world swirling
by in miraculous limousines; legless cripples flopping
on hands and leather pads; thin-whiskered stu-
dents in velveteen; walrus-moustached veterans in
broadcloth; keen-faced old prelates; shabby young
priests; cavalrymen in casque and cuirass; work-
ingmen turned horse and harnessed to carts; sidewalk jesters, itinerant vendors of questionable
wares; shady loafers dressed to resemble gold-
showering America; motor-cyclists in leather; hairy
musicians, blue gendarmes, baggy red zouaves; purple-

faced, glazed-hatted, scarlet-waistcoated, cigarette-
smoking cabmen, calling one another "onions,"
"camels," and names even more terrible. Women
prevalent over all the concourse; fair women, dark
women, pretty women, gilded women, haughty
women, indifferent women, friendly women, merry
women. Fine women in fine clothes; rich women in
fine clothes; poor women in fine clothes. Worldly
old women, reclining befurred in electric landaulettes;
wordy old women hoydenishly trundling carts full
of flowers. Wonderful automobile women quick-
glimpsed, in multiple veils of white and brown and
sea-green. Women in rags and tags, and women
draped, coifed, and befrilled in the delirium of
maddened poet-milliners and the hasheesh dreams
of ladies' tailors.

About the procession, as it moves interminably
along the boulevard, a blue haze of fine dust and
burnt gasoline rises into the sunshine like the haze
over the passages to an amphitheatre toward which
a crowd is trampling; and through this the multitudes seem to go as actors passing to their cues.
Your place at one of the little tables upon the sidewalk is that of a wayside spectator: and as the
performers go by, in some measure acting or look-

ing their parts already, as if in preparation, you guess the rôles they play, and name them comedians, tragedians, buffoons, saints, beauties, sots, knaves, gladiators, acrobats, dancers; for all of these are there, and you distinguish the principles from the unnumbered supernumeraries pressing forward to the entrances. So, if you sit at the little tables often enough—that is, if you become an amateur boulevardier—you begin to recognise the transient stars of the pageant, those to whom the boulevard allows a dubious and fugitive rôle of celebrity, and whom it greets with a slight flutter: the turning of heads, a murmur of comment, and the incredulous boulevard smile, which seems to say: "You see? Madame and monsieur passing there—evidently they think we still believe in them!"

This flutter heralded and followed the passing of a white touring-car with the procession one afternoon, just before the Grand Prix, though it needed no boulevard celebrity to make the man who lolled in the tonneau conspicuous. Simply for *that*, notoriety was superfluous; so were the remarkable size and power of his car; so was the elaborate touring-costume of flannels and pongee he wore; so was even the enamelled presence of the dancer who sat beside him. His face would have done it without accessories.

My old friend, George Ward, and I had met for our *apéritif* at the Terrace Larue, by the Madeleine, when the white automobile came snaking its way craftily through the traffic. Turning in to pass a victoria on the wrong side, it was forced down to a snail's pace near the curb and not far from our table, where it paused, checked by a blockade at the next corner. I heard Ward utter a half-suppressed guttural of what I took to be amazement, and I did not wonder.

The face of the man in the tonneau detached him to the spectator's gaze and singled him out of the concourse with an effect almost ludicrous in its incongruity. The hair was dark, lustrous and thick, the forehead broad and finely modelled, and certain other ruinous vestiges of youth and good looks remained; but whatever the features might once have shown of honour, worth, or kindly semblance had disappeared beyond all tracing in a blurred distortion. The lids of one eye were discoloured and swollen almost together; other traces of a recent battering were not lacking, nor was cosmetic evidence of a heroic struggle, on the part of some valet of infinite pains, to efface them. The nose lost outline in the discolorations of the puffed cheeks; the chin, tufted with a small imperial, trembled beneath a sagging, gray lip. And that this bruised and dissipated mask should suffer the final grotesque touch, it was decorated with the moustache of a coquettish marquis, the ends waxed and exquisitely elevated.

The figure was fat, but loose and sprawling, seemingly without the will to hold itself together; in truth the man appeared to be almost in a semi-stupor, and, contrasted with this powdered Silenus, even the woman beside him gained something of human dignity. At least, she was thoroughly alive, bold, predatory, and in spite of the gross embon-point that threatened her, still savagely graceful. A purple veil, dotted with gold, floated about her hat, from which green-dyed ostrich plumes cascaded down across a cheek enamelled dead white. Her hair was plastered in blue-black waves, parted low on the forehead; her lips were splashed a startling carmine, the eyelids painted blue; and, from between lashes gummed into little spikes of blacking, she favoured her companion with a glance of carelessly simulated tenderness,—a look all too

vividly suggesting the ghastly calculations of a
cook wheedling a chicken nearer the kitchen door.
But I felt no great pity for the victim.

"Who is it?" I asked, staring at the man in the
automobile and not turning toward Ward.

"That is Mariana—'*la bella Mariana la Mursiana,*'" George answered; "—one of those women
who come to Paris from the tropics to form themselves on the legend of the one great famous and
infamous Spanish dancer who died a long while
ago. Mariana did very well for a time. I've heard
that the revolutionary societies intend striking
medals in her honour: she's done worse things to
royalty than all the anarchists in Europe! But her
great days are over: she's getting old; that type
goes to pieces quickly, once it begins to slump,
and it won't be long before she'll be horribly fat,
though she's still a graceful dancer. She danced
at the Folie Rouge last week."

"Thank you, George," I said gratefully. "I
hope you'll point out the Louvre and the Eiffel
Tower to me some day. I didn't mean Mariana."

"What did you mean?"

What I had meant was so obvious that I turned
to my friend in surprise. He was nervously tapping

his chin with the handle of his cane and staring at the white automobile with very grim interest.

"I meant the man with her," I said.

"Oh!" He laughed sourly. "That carrion?"

"You seem to be an acquaintance."

"Everybody on the boulevard knows who he is," said Ward curtly, paused, and laughed again with very little mirth. "So do you," he continued; "and as for my acquaintance with him—yes, I had once the distinction of being his rival in a small way, a way so small, in fact, that it ended in his becoming a connection of mine by marriage. He's Larrabee Harman."

That was a name somewhat familiar to readers of American newspapers even before its bearer was fairly out of college. The publicity it then attained (partly due to young Harman's conspicuous wealth) attached to some youthful exploits not without a certain wild humour. But frolic degenerated into brawl and debauch: what had been scrapes for the boy became scandals for the man; and he gathered a more and more unsavoury reputation until its like was not to be found outside a penitentiary. The crux of his career in his own country was reached during a midnight quarrel in Chicago when he shot a negro gambler. After that, the negro having recovered and the matter being somehow arranged so that the prosecution was dropped, Harman's wife left him, and the papers recorded her application for a divorce. She was George Ward's second cousin, the daughter of a Baltimore clergyman; a belle in a season and town of belles, and a delightful, headstrong creature, from all accounts. She had made a runaway match of it with Harman three years before, their affair having been earnestly opposed by all her relatives—especially by poor George, who came over to Paris just after the wedding in a miserable frame of mind.

The Chicago exploit was by no means the end of Harman's notoriety. Evading an effort (on the part of an aunt, I believe) to get him locked up safely in a "sanitarium," he began a trip round the world with an orgy which continued from San Francisco to Bangkok, where, in the company of some congenial fellow travellers, he interfered in a native ceremonial with the result that one of his companions was drowned. Proceeding, he was reported to be in serious trouble at Constantinople, the result of an inquisitiveness little appreciated by Orientals. The State Department, bestirring itself, saved him from a very real peril, and he continued his journey. In Rome he was rescued with difficulty from a street mob that unreasonably refused to accept intoxication as an excuse for his riding down a child on his way to the hunt. Later, during the winter just past, we had been hearing from Monte Carlo of his disastrous plunges at that most imbecile of all games, roulette.

Every event, no matter how trifling, in this man's pitiful career had been recorded in the American newspapers with an elaboration which, for my part, I found infuriatingly tiresome. I have lived in Paris so long that I am afraid to go home: I have too little to show for my years of pottering with paint and canvas, and I have grown timid about all the changes that have crept in at home. I do not know the "new men," I do not know how they would use me, and fear they might make no place for me; and so I fit myself more closely into the little grooves I have worn for myself, and resign myself to stay. But I am no "*expatriate*." I know there is a feeling at home against us who remain over here to do our work, but in most instances it is a prejudice which springs from a misunderstanding. I think the quality of patriotism

in those of us who "didn't go home in time" is
almost pathetically deep and real, and, like many
another oldish fellow in my position, I try to keep
as close to things at home as I can. All of my
old friends gradually ceased to write to me, but
I still take three home newspapers, trying to follow the people I knew and the things that happen;
and the ubiquity of so worthless a creature as
Larrabee Harman in the columns I dredged for
real news had long been a point of irritation to
this present exile. Not only that: he had usurped
space in the Continental papers, and of late my
favourite Parisian journal had served him to me
with my morning coffee, only hinting his name, but
offering him with that gracious satire character-
istic of the Gallic journalist writing of anything
American. And so this grotesque wreck of a man
was well known to the boulevard—one of its sights.
That was to be perceived by the flutter he caused,
by the turning of heads in his direction, and the
low laughter of the people at the little tables. Three
or four in the rear ranks had risen to their feet
to get a better look at him and his companion.

Some one behind us chuckled aloud. "They say
Mariana beats him."

"Evidently!"

The dancer was aware of the flutter, and called Harman's attention to it with a touch upon his arm and a laugh and a nod of her violent plumage.

At that he seemed to rouse himself somewhat: his head rolled heavily over upon his shoulder, the lids lifted a little from the red-shot eyes, showing a strange pride when his gaze fell upon the many staring faces.

Then, as the procession moved again and the white automobile with it, the sottish mouth widened in a smile of dull and cynical contempt: the look of a half-poisoned Augustan borne down through the crowds from the Palatine after supping with Caligula.

Ward pulled my sleeve.

"Come," he said, "let us go over to the Luxembourg gardens where the air is cleaner."

CHAPTER II

WARD is a portrait-painter, and in the matter of vogue there seem to be no pinnacles left for him to surmount. I think he has painted most of the very rich women of fashion who have come to Paris of late years, and he has become so prosperous, has such a polite celebrity, and his opinions upon art are so conclusively quoted, that the friendship of some of us who started with him has been dangerously strained.

He lives a well-ordered life; he has always led that kind of life. Even in his student days when I first knew him, I do not remember an occasion upon which the principal of a New England high-school would have criticised his conduct. And yet I never heard anyone call him a prig; and, so far as I know, no one was ever so stupid as to think him one. He was a quiet, good-looking, well-dressed boy, and he matured into a somewhat reserved, well-poised man, of impressive distinction in appearance and manner. He has always been

well tended and cared for by women; in his student days his mother lived with him; his sister,
Miss Elizabeth, looks after him now. She came
with him when he returned to Paris after his disappointment in the unfortunate Harman affair, and
she took charge of all his business—as well as his
social—arrangements (she has been accused of a
theory that the two things may be happily combined), making him lease a house in an expensively
modish quarter near the Avenue du Bois de
Boulogne. Miss Elizabeth is an instinctively fashionable woman, practical withal, and to her mind
success should be not only respectable but "smart."
She does not speak of the "right bank" and the
"left bank" of the Seine; she calls them the "right
bank" and the "wrong bank." And yet, though
she removed George (her word is "rescued") from
many of his old associations with Montparnasse,
she warmly encouraged my friendship with him—
yea, in spite of my living so deep in the wrong
bank that the first time he brought her to my
studio, she declared she hadn't seen anything
so like Bring-the-child-to-the-old-hag's-cellar-at-mid-
night since her childhood. She is a handsome
woman, large, and of a fine, high colour; her manner

is gaily dictatorial, and she and I got along very well together.

Probably she appreciated my going to some pains with the clothes I wore when I went to their house. My visits there were infrequent, not because I had any fear of wearing out a welcome, but on account of Miss Elizabeth's "day," when I could see nothing of George for the crowd of lionising women and time-wasters about him. Her "day" was a dread of mine; I could seldom remember which day it was, and when I did she had a way of shifting it so that I was fatally sure to run into it—to my misery, for, beginning with those primordial indignities suffered in youth, when I was scrubbed with a handkerchief outside the parlour door as a preliminary to polite usages, my childhood's, manhood's prayer has been: From all such days, Good Lord, deliver me!

It was George's habit to come much oftener to see me. He always really liked the sort of society his sister had brought about him; but now and then there were intervals when it wore on him a little, I think. Sometimes he came for me in his automobile and we would make a mild excursion to breakfast in the country; and that is what happened one morning about three weeks after the day when we had sought pure air in the Luxembourg gardens.

We drove out through the Bois and by Suresnes, striking into a roundabout road to Versailles beyond St. Cloud. It was June, a dustless and balmy noon, the air thinly gilded by a faint haze, and I know few things pleasanter than that road on a fair day of the early summer and no sweeter way to course it than in an open car; though I must not be giving myself out for a "motorist" —I have not even the right cap. I am usually nervous in big machines, too; but Ward has never caught the speed mania and holds a strange power over his chauffeur; so we rolled along peacefully, not madly, and smoked (like the car) in hasteless content.

"After all," said George, with a placid wave of the hand, "I sometimes wish that the landscape had called me. You outdoor men have all the health and pleasure of living in the open, and as for the work—oh! you fellows think you work, but you don't know what it means."

"No?" I said, and smiled as I always meanly do when George "talks art." He was silent for a few moments and then said irritably,

"Well, at least you can't deny that the academic crowd can DRAW!"

Never having denied it, though he had challenged me in the same way perhaps a thousand times, I refused to deny it now; whereupon he returned to his theme: "Landscape is about as simple as a stage fight; two up, two down, cross and repeat. Take that ahead of us. Could anything be simpler to paint?"

He indicated the white road running before us between open fields to a curve, where it descended to pass beneath an old stone culvert. Beyond, stood a thick grove with a clear sky flickering among the branches. An old peasant woman was pushing a heavy cart round the curve, a scarlet handkerchief knotted about her head.

"You think it's easy?" I asked.

"Easy! Two hours ought to do it as well as it could be done—at least, the way you fellows do it!" He clenched his fingers as if upon the handle of a house-painter's brush. "Slap, dash— there's your road." He paddled the air with the imaginary brush as though painting the side of a barn. "Swish, swash—there go your fields and your stone bridge. Fit! Speck! And there's your

old woman, her red handkerchief, and what your
dealer will probably call 'the human interest,' all
complete. Squirt the edges of your foliage in with
a blow-pipe. Throw a cup of tea over the whole,
and there's your haze. Call it 'The Golden Road,'
or 'The Bath of Sunlight,' or 'Quiet Noon.' Then
you'll probably get a criticism beginning, 'Few indeed have more intangibly detained upon canvas
so poetic a quality of sentiment as this sterling
landscapist, who in Number 136 has most ethereally
expressed the profound silence of evening on an
English moor. The solemn hush, the brooding
quiet, the homeward ploughman——' "

He was interrupted by an outrageous uproar,
the grisly scream of a siren and the cannonade of
a powerful exhaust, as a great white touring-car
swung round us from behind at a speed that sick-
ened me to see, and, snorting thunder, passed us
"as if we had been standing still."

It hurtled like a comet down the curve and we
were instantly choking in its swirling tail of dust.

"Seventy miles an hour!" gasped George, swab-
bing at his eyes. "Those are the fellows that get
into the pa— Oh, Lord! *There* they go!"

Swinging out to pass us and then sweeping in

upon the reverse curve to clear the narrow arch of the culvert were too much for the white car; and through the dust we saw it rock dangerously. In the middle of the road, ten feet from the culvert, the old woman struggled frantically to get her cart out of the way. The howl of the siren frightened her perhaps, for she lost her head and went to the wrong side. Then the shriek of the machine drowned the human scream as the automobile struck.

The shock of contact was muffled. But the mass of machinery hoisted itself in the air as if it had a life of its own and had been stung into sudden madness. It was horrible to see, and so grotesque that a long-forgotten memory of my boyhood leaped instantaneously into my mind, a recollection of the evolutions performed by a Newfoundland dog that rooted under a board walk and found a hive of wild bees.

The great machine left the road for the fields on the right, reared, fell, leaped against the stone side of the culvert, apparently trying to climb it, stood straight on end, whirled backward in a half-somersault, crashed over on its side, flashed with flame and explosion, and lay hidden under a cloud of dust and smoke.

Ward's driver slammed down his accelerator, sent us spinning round the curve, and the next moment, throwing on his brakes, halted sharply at the culvert.

The fabric of the road was so torn and distorted one might have thought a steam dredge had begun work there, but the fragments of wreckage were oddly isolated and inconspicuous. The peasant's cart, tossed into a clump of weeds, rested on its side, the spokes of a rimless wheel slowly revolving on the hub uppermost. Some tools were strewn in a semi-circular trail in the dust; a pair of smashed goggles crunched beneath my foot as I sprang out of Ward's car, and a big brass lamp had fallen in the middle of the road, crumpled like waste paper. Beside it lay a gold rouge box.

The old woman had somehow saved herself—or perhaps her saint had helped her—for she was sitting in the grass by the roadside, wailing hysterically and quite unhurt. The body of a man lay in a heap beneath the stone archway, and from his clothes I guessed that he had been the driver of the white car. I say "had been" because there were reasons for needing no second glance to comprehend that the man was dead. Nevertheless, I knelt beside him and placed my hand upon his breast to see if his heart still beat. Afterward I concluded that I did this because I had seen it done upon the stage, or had read of it in stories; and even at the time I realised that it was a silly thing for me to be doing.

Ward, meanwhile, proved more practical. He was dragging a woman out of the suffocating smoke and dust that shrouded the wreck, and after a moment I went to help him carry her into the fresh air, where George put his coat under her head. Her hat had been forced forward over her face and held there by the twisting of a system of veils she wore; and we had some difficulty in unravelling this; but she was very much alive, as a series of muffled imprecations testified, leading us to conclude that her sufferings were more profoundly of rage than of pain. Finally she pushed our hands angrily aside and completed the untanglement herself, revealing the scratched and smeared face of Mariana, the dancer.

"*Cornichon! Chameau! Fond du bain!*" she gasped, tears of anger starting from her eyes. She tried to rise before we could help her, but dropped back with a scream.

"Oh, the pain!" she cried. "That imbecile! If he has let me break my leg! A pretty dancer I should be! I hope he is killed."

One of the singularities of motoring on the main-travelled roads near Paris is the prevalence of cars containing physicians and surgeons. Whether it be testimony to the opportunism, to the sporting proclivities, or to the prosperity of gentlemen of those professions, I do not know, but it is a fact that I have never heard of an accident (and in the season there is an accident every day) on one of these roads when a doctor in an automobile was not almost immediately a chance arrival, and fortunately our case offered no exception to this rule. Another automobile had already come up and the occupants were hastily alighting. Ward shouted to the foremost to go for a doctor.

"I am a doctor," the man answered, advancing and kneeling quickly by the dancer. "And you— you may be of help yonder."

We turned toward the ruined car where Ward's driver was shouting for us.

"What is it?" called Ward as we ran toward him.

"Monsieur," he replied, "there is some one under the tonneau here!"

The smoke had cleared a little, though a rivulet of burning gasoline ran from the wreck to a pool of flame it was feeding in the road. The front cushions and woodwork had caught fire and a couple of labourers, panting with the run across the fields, were vainly belabouring the flames with brushwood. From beneath the overturned tonneau projected the lower part of a man's leg, clad in a brown puttee and a russet shoe. Ward's driver had brought his tools; had jacked up the car as high as possible; but was still unable to release the imprisoned body.

"I have seized that foot and pulled with all my strength," he said, "and I cannot make him move one centimetre. It is necessary that as many people as possible lay hold of the car on the side away from the fire and all lift together. Yes," he added, "and very soon!"

Some carters had come from the road and one of them lay full length on the ground peering beneath the wreck. "It is the head of monsieur," explained this one; "it is the head of monsieur which is fastened under there."

"Eh, but you are wiser than Clémenceau!" said the chauffeur. "Get up, my ancient, and you there, with the brushwood, let the fire go for a moment and help, when I say the word. And you, monsieur," he turned to Ward, "if you please, will you pull with me upon the ankle here at the right moment?"

The carters, the labourers, the men from the other automobile, and I laid hold of the car together.

"Now, then, messieurs, LIFT!"

Stifled with the gasoline smoke, we obeyed. One or two hands were scorched and our eyes smarted blindingly, but we gave a mighty heave, and felt the car rising.

"Well done!" cried the chauffeur. "Well done! But a little more! The smallest fraction—HA! It is finished, messieurs!"

We staggered back, coughing and wiping our eyes. For a minute or two I could not see at all, and was busy with a handkerchief.

Ward laid his hand on my shoulder.

"Do you know who it is?" he asked.

"Yes, of course," I answered.

When I could see again, I found that I was looking almost straight down into the upturned face of Larrabee Harman, and I cannot better express what this man had come to be, and what the degradation of his life had written upon him, than by saying that the dreadful thing I looked upon now was no more horrible a sight than the face I had seen, fresh from the valet and smiling in ugly pride at the starers, as he passed the terrace of Larue on the day before the Grand Prix.

We helped to carry him to the doctor's car, and to lift the dancer into Ward's, and to get both of them out again at the hospital at Versailles, where they were taken. Then, with no need to ask each other if we should abandon our plan to breakfast in the country, we turned toward Paris, and rolled along almost to the barriers in silence.

"Did it seem to you," said George finally, "that a man so frightfully injured could have any chance of getting well?"

"No," I answered. "I thought he was dying as we carried him into the hospital."

"So did I. The top of his head seemed all crushed in—Whew!" He broke off, shivering, and wiped his brow. After a pause he added thoughtfully, "It will be a great thing for Louise."

Louise was the name of his second cousin, the girl who had done battle with all her family and then run away from them to be Larrabee Harman's wife. Remembering the stir that her application for divorce had made, I did not understand how Harman's death could benefit her, unless George had some reason to believe that he had made a will in her favour. However, the remark had been made more to himself than to me and I did not respond.

The morning papers flared once more with the name of Larrabee Harman, and we read that there was "no hope of his surviving." Ironic phrase! There was not a soul on earth that day who could have hoped for his recovery, or who—for his sake —cared two straws whether he lived or died. And the dancer had been right; one of her legs was badly broken: she would never dance again.

Evening papers reported that Harman was "lingering." He was lingering the next day. He was lingering the next week, and the end of a month saw him still "lingering." Then I went down to Capri, where—for he had been after all the merest episode to me—I was pleased to forget all about him.

CHAPTER III

A GREAT many people keep their friends in mind by writing to them, but more do not; and Ward and I belong to the majority. After my departure from Paris I had but one missive from him, a short note, written at the request of his sister, asking me to be on the lookout for Italian earrings, to add to her collection of old jewels. So, from time to time, I sent her what I could find about Capri or in Naples, and she responded with neat little letters of acknowledgment.

Two years I stayed on Capri, eating the lotus which grows on that happy island, and painting very little—only enough, indeed, to be remembered at the Salon and not so much as knowing how kindly or unkindly they hung my pictures there. But even on Capri, people sometimes hear the call of Paris and wish to be in that unending movement: to hear the multitudinous rumble, to watch the procession from a café terrace and to dine at Foyot's. So there came at last a fine day when I, knowing that the horse-chestnuts were in bloom along the Champs Elysées, threw my rope-soled shoes to a beggar, packed a rusty trunk, and was off for the banks of the Seine.

My arrival—just the drive from the Gare de Lyon to my studio—was like the shock of surf on a bather's breast.

The stir and life, the cheerful energy of the streets, put stir and life and cheerful energy into me. I felt the itch to work again, to be at it, at it in earnest—to lose no hour of daylight, and to paint better than I had painted!

Paris having given me this impetus, I dared not tempt her further, nor allow the edge of my eagerness time to blunt; therefore, at the end of a fortnight, I went over into Normandy and deposited that rusty trunk of mine in a corner of the summer pavilion in the courtyard of Madame Brossard's inn, *Les Trois Pigeons*, in a woodland neighborhood that is there. Here I had painted through a prolific summer of my youth, and I was glad to find—as I had hoped—nothing changed; for the place was dear to me. Madame Brossard (dark, thin, demure as of yore, a fine-looking woman with a fine manner and much the flavour of old Norman

portraits) gave me a pleasant welcome, remembering me readily but without surprise, while Amédée,
the antique servitor, cackled over me and was as
proud of my advent as if I had been a new egg and
he had laid me. The simile is grotesque; but Amédée
is the most henlike waiter in France.

He is a white-haired, fat old fellow, always well-
shaved; as neat as a billiard-ball. In the daytime,
when he is partly porter, he wears a black tie, a
gray waistcoat broadly striped with scarlet, and,
from waist to feet, a white apron like a skirt, and
so competently encircling that his trousers are of
mere conventionality and no real necessity; but
after six o'clock (becoming altogether a maître
d'hôtel) he is clad as any other formal gentleman.
At all times he wears a fresh table-cloth over his
arm, keeping an exaggerated pile of them ready
at hand on a ledge in one of the little bowers of
the courtyard, so that he may never be shamed
by getting caught without one.

His conception of life is that all worthy persons
were created as receptacles for food and drink; and
five minutes after my arrival he had me seated (in
spite of some meek protests) in a wicker chair with
a pitcher of the right Three Pigeons cider on the

table before me, while he subtly dictated what manner of dinner I should eat. For this interval Amédée's exuburance was sobered and his bandinage dismissed as being mere garniture, the questions now before us concerning grave and inward matters. His suggestions were deferential but insistent; his manner was that of a prime minister who goes through the form of convincing the sovereign. He greeted each of his own decisions with a very loud "*Bien!*" as if startled by the brilliancy of my selections, and, the menu being concluded, exploded a whole volley of "*Biens*" and set off violently to instruct old Gaston, the cook.

That is Amédée's way; he always starts violently for anywhere he means to go. He is a little lame and his progress more or less sidelong, but if you call him, or new guests arrive at the inn, or he receives an order from Madame Brossard, he gives the effect of running by a sudden movement of the whole body like that of a man *about* to run, and moves off using the gestures of a man who *is* running; after which he proceeds to his destination at an exquisite leisure. Remembering this old habit of his, it was with joy that I noted his headlong departure. Some ten feet of his progress accomplished, he halted (for no purpose but to scratch his head the more luxuriously); next, strayed from the path to contemplate a rose-bush, and, selecting a leaf with careful deliberation, placed it in his mouth and continued meditatively upon his way to the kitchen.

I chuckled within me; it was good to be back at Madame Brossard's.

The courtyard was more a garden; bright with rows of flowers in formal little beds and blossoming up from big green tubs, from red jars, and also from two brightly painted wheel-barrows. A long arbour offered a shelter of vines for those who might choose to dine, breakfast, or lounge beneath, and, here and there among the shrubberies, you might come upon a latticed bower, thatched with straw. My own pavilion (half bedroom, half studio) was set in the midst of all and had a small porch of its own with a rich curtain of climbing honeysuckle for a screen from the rest of the courtyard.

The inn itself is gray with age, the roof sagging pleasantly here and there; and an old wooden gallery runs the length of each wing, the guest-chambers of the upper story opening upon it like the deck-rooms of a steamer, with boxes of tulips and hyacinths along the gallery railings and window ledges for the gayest of border-lines.

Beyond the great open archway, which gives entrance to the courtyard, lies the quiet country road; passing this, my eyes followed the wide sweep of poppy-sprinkled fields to a line of low green hills; and there was the edge of the forest sheltering those woodland interiors which I had long ago tried to paint, and where I should be at work to-morrow.

In the course of time, and well within the bright twilight, Amédée spread the crisp white cloth and served me at a table on my pavilion porch. He feigned anxiety lest I should find certain dishes (those which he knew were most delectable) not to my taste, but was obviously so distended with fatuous pride over the whole meal that it became a temptation to denounce at least some trifling sauce or garnishment; nevertheless, so much mendacity proved beyond me and I spared him and my own conscience. This puffed-uppedness of his was to be observed only in his expression of manner, for during the consumption of food it was his worthy custom to practise a ceremonious, nay, a reverential,

hush, and he never offered (or approved) conversation until he had prepared the salad. That
accomplished, however, and the water bubbling in
the coffee machine, he readily favoured me with
a discourse on the decline in glory of *Les Trois
Pigeons.*

"Monsieur, it is the automobiles; they have done
it. Formerly, as when monsieur was here, the
painters came from Paris. They would come in
the spring and would stay until the autumn rains.
What busy times and what drolleries! Ah, it was
gay in those days! Monsieur remembers well.
Ha, Ha! But now, I think, the automobiles have
frightened away the painters; at least they do not
come any more. And the automobiles themselves;
they come sometimes for lunch, a few, but they
love better the seashore, and we are just close
enough to be too far away. Those automobiles,
they love the big new hotels and the casinos with
roulette. They eat hastily, gulp down a liqueur,
and *pouf!* off they rush for Trouville, for Houlgate
—for heaven knows where! And even the automobiles do not come so frequenlty as they did. Our
road used to be the best from Lisieux to Beuzeval,
but now the maps recommend another. They pass

us by, and yet yonder—only a few kilometres—is the coast with its thousands. We are near the world but out of it, monsieur."

He poured my coffee; dropped a lump of sugar from the tongs with a benevolent gesture—"One lump: always the same. Monsieur sees that I remember well, ha?"—and the twilight having fallen, he lit two orange-shaded candles and my cigar with the same match. The night was so quiet that the candle-lights burned as steadily as flames in a globe, yet the air was spiced with a cool fragrance, and through the honeysuckle leaves above me I saw, as I leaned back in my wicker chair, a glimmer of kindly stars.

"Very comfortably out of the world, Amédée," I said. "It seems to me I have it all to myself."

"Unhappily, yes!" he exclaimed; then excused himself, chuckling. "I should have said that we should be happier if we had many like monsieur. But it is early in the season to despair. Then, too, our best suite is already engaged."

"By whom?"

"Two men of science who arrive next week. One is a great man. Madame Brossard is pleased that he is coming to *Les Trois Pigeons*, but I tell her it is only natural. He comes now for the first time because he likes the quiet, but he will come again, like monsieur, because he has been here before. That is what I always say: 'Any one who has been here must come again.' The problem is only to get them to come the first time. Truly!"

"Who is the great man, Amédée?"

"Ah! A distinguished professor of science. Truly."

"What science?"

"I do not know. But he is a member of the Institute. Monsieur must have heard of that great Professor Keredec?"

"The name is known. Who is the other?"

"A friend of his. I do not know. All the upper floor of the east wing they have taken—the Grande Suite—those two and their valet-de-chambre. That is truly the way in modern times—the philosophers are rich men."

"Yes," I sighed. "Only the painters are poor nowadays."

"Ha, ha, monsieur!" Amédée laughed cunningly. "It was always easy to see that monsieur only amuses himself with his painting."

"Thank you, Amédée," I responded. "I have amused other people with it too, I fear."

"Oh, without doubt!" he agreed graciously, as he folded the cloth. I have always tried to believe that it was not so much my pictures as the fact that I paid my bills the day they were presented which convinced everybody about *Les Trois Pigeons* that I was an amateur. But I never became happily enough settled in this opinion to risk pressing an investigation; and it was a relief that Amédée changed the subject.

"Monsieur remembers the Château de Quesnay —at the crest of the hill on the road north of Dives?"

"I remember."

"It is occupied this season by some rich Americans."

"How do you know they are rich?"

"*Dieu de Dieu!*" The old fellow appealed to heaven. "But they are Americans!"

"And therefore millionaires. Perfectly, Amédée."

"Perfectly, monsieur. Perhaps monsieur knows them."

"Yes, I know them."

"Truly!" He affected dejection. "And poor Madame Brossard thought monsieur had returned to our old hotel because he liked it, and remembered our wine of Beaune and the good beds and old Gaston's cooking!"

"Do not weep, Amédée," I said. "I have come to paint; not because I know the people who have taken Quesnay." And I added: "I may not see them at all."

In truth I thought that very probable. Miss Elizabeth had mentioned in one of her notes that Ward had leased Quesnay, but I had not sought quarters at *Les Trois Pigeons* because it stood within walking distance of the château. In my industrious frame of mind that circumstance seemed almost a drawback. Miss Elizabeth, ever hospitable to those whom she noticed at all, would be doubly so in the country, as people always are; and I wanted all my time to myself—no very selfish wish since my time was not conceivably of value to any one else. I thought it wise to leave any encounter with the lady to chance, and as the by-paths of the country-side were many and intricate, I intended, without ungallantry, to render the chance remote. George himself had just sailed on a business trip to America, as I knew from her last missive; and until his return, I should put in all my time at painting and nothing else, though

I liked his sister, as I have said, and thought of her—often.

Amédée doubted my sincerity, however, for he laughed incredulously.

"Eh, well, monsieur enjoys saying it!"

"Certainly. It is a pleasure to say what one means."

"But monsieur could not mean it. Monsieur will call at the château in the morning"—the complacent varlet prophesied—"as early as it will be polite. I am sure of that. Monsieur is not at all an old man; no, not yet! Even if he were, aha! no one could possess the friendship of that wonderful Madame d'Armand and remain away from the château."

"Madame d'Armand?" I said. "That is not the name. You mean Mademoiselle Ward."

"No, no!" He shook his head and his fat cheeks bulged with a smile which I believe he intended to express a respectful roguishness. "Mademoiselle Ward" (he pronounced it "Ware") "is magnificent; every one must fly to obey when she opens her mouth. If she did not like the ocean there below the château, the ocean would have to move! It needs only a glance to perceive that Mademoiselle Ward is a great lady—but *Madame d'Ar-mand!* AHA!" He rolled his round eyes to an effect of unspeakable admiration, and with a gesture indicated that he would have kissed his hand to the stars, had that been properly reverential to Madame d'Armand. "But monsieur knows very well for himself!"

"Monsieur knows that you are very confusing— even for a maître d'hôtel. We were speaking of the present chatelaine of Quesnay, Mademoiselle Ward. I have never heard of Madame d'Armand."

"Monsieur is serious?"

"Truly!" I answered, making bold to quote his shibboleth.

"Then monsieur has truly much to live for. Truly!" he chuckled openly, convinced that he had obtained a marked advantage in a conflict of wits, shaking his big head from side to side with an exasperating air of knowingness. "Ah, truly! When that lady drives by, some day, in the carriage from the château—eh? Then monsieur will see how much he has to live for. Truly, truly, truly!"

He had cleared the table, and now, with a final explosion of the word which gave him such immoderate satisfaction, he lifted the tray and made one of his precipitate departures.

"Amédée," I said, as he slackened down to his sidelong leisure.

"Monsieur?"

"Who is Madame d'Armand?"

"A guest of Mademoiselle Ward at Quesnay. In fact, she is in charge of the château, since Mademoiselle Ward is, for the time, away."

"Is she a Frenchwoman?"

"It seems not. In fact, she is an American, though she dresses with so much of taste. Ah, Madame Brossard admits it, and Madame Brossard knows the art of dressing, for she spends a week of every winter in Rouen—and besides there is Trouville itself only some kilometres distant. Madame Brossard says that Mademoiselle Ward dresses with richness and splendour and Madame d'Armand with economy, but beauty. Those were the words used by Madame Brossard. Truly."

"Madame d'Armand's name is French," I observed.

"Yes, that is true," said Amédée thoughtfully. "No one can deny it; it is a French name." He rested the tray upon a stump near by and scratched his head. "I do not understand how that can be," he continued slowly. "Jean Ferret, who is chief gardener at the château, is an acquaintance of mine. We sometimes have a cup of cider at Père Baudry's, a kilometre down the road from here; and Jean Ferret has told me that she is an American. And yet, as you say, monsieur, the name is French. Perhaps she is French after all."

"I believe," said I, "that if I struggled a few days over this puzzle, I might come to the conclusion that Madame d'Armand is an American lady who has married a Frenchman."

The old man uttered an exclamation of triumph.

"Ha! without doubt! Truly she must be an American lady who has married a Frenchman. Monsieur has already solved the puzzle. Truly, truly!" And he trulied himself across the darkness, to emerge in the light of the open door of the kitchen with the word still rumbling in his throat.

Now for a time there came the clinking of dishes, sounds as of pans and kettles being scoured, the rolling gutturals of old Gaston, the cook, and the treble pipings of young "Glouglou," his grandchild and scullion. After a while the oblong of light from the kitchen door disappeared; the voices

departed; the stillness of the dark descended, and
with it that unreasonable sense of pathos which
night in the country brings to the heart of a wan-
derer. Then, out of the lonely silence, there issued
a strange, incongruous sound as an execrable voice
essayed to produce the semblance of an air odiously
familiar about the streets of Paris some three years
past, and I became aware of a smell of some dreadful thing burning. Beneath the arbour I perceived
a glowing spark which seemed to bear a certain
relation to an oval whitish patch suggesting the
front of a shirt. It was Amédée, at ease, smoking
his cigarette after the day's work and convinced
that he was singing.

> *"Pour qu'j'finisse*
> *Mon service*
> *Au Tonkin je suis parti——*
> *Ah! quel beau pays, mesdames!*
> *C'est l'paradis des p'tites femmes!"*

I rose from the chair on my little porch, to go
to bed; but I was reminded of something, and
called to him.

"Monsieur?" his voice came briskly.

"How often do you see your friend, Jean Ferret, the gardener of Quesnay?"

"Frequently, monsieur. To-morrow morning I could easily carry a message if——"

"That is precisely what I do not wish. And you may as well not mention me at all when you meet him."

"It is understood. Perfectly."

"If it is well understood, there will be a beautiful present for a good maître d'hôtel some day."

"Thank you, monsieur."

"Good night, Amédée."

"Good night, monsieur."

.   .   .   —   .   .

Falling to sleep has always been an intricate matter with me: I liken it to a nightly adventure in an enchanted palace. Weary-limbed and with burning eyelids, after long waiting in the outer court of wakefulness, I enter a dim, cool antechamber where the heavy garment of the body is left behind and where, perhaps, some acquaintance or friend greets me with a familiar speech or a bit of nonsense—or an unseen orchestra may play music that I know. From here I go into a spacious apartment where the air and light are of a fine clarity, for it is the hall of revelations, and in it the secrets of secrets are told, mysteries are resolved, perplexities cleared up, and sometimes I learn what to do about a picture that has bothered me. This is where I would linger, for beyond it I walk among crowding fantasies, delusions, terrors and shame, to a curtain of darkness where they take my memory from me, and I know nothing of my own adventures until I am pushed out of a secret door into the morning sunlight. Amédée was the acquaintance who met me in the antechamber to-night. He remarked that Madame d'Armand was the most beautiful woman in the world, and vanished. And in the hall of revelations I thought that I found a statue of her—but it was veiled. I wished to remove the veil, but a passing stranger stopped and told me laughingly that the veil was all that would ever be revealed of her to me—of her, or any other woman!

CHAPTER IV

I WAS up with the birds in the morning; had my breakfast with them—a very drowsy-eyed Amédée assisting—and made off for the forest to get the sunrise through the branches, a pack on my back and three sandwiches for lunch in my pocket. I returned only with the failing light of evening, cheerfully tired and ready for a fine dinner and an early bed, both of which the good inn supplied. It was my daily programme; a healthy life "far from the world," as Amédée said, and I was sorry when the serpent entered and disturbed it, though he was my own. He is a pet of mine; has been with me since my childhood. He leaves me when I live alone, for he loves company, but returns whenever my kind are about me. There are many names for snakes of his breed, but, to deal charitably with myself, I call mine Interest-In-Other-People's-Affairs.

One evening I returned to find a big van from Dives, the nearest railway station, drawn up in the courtyard at the foot of the stairs leading to the

47

gallery, and all of the people of the inn, from Madame Brossard (who directed) to Glouglou (who madly attempted the heaviest pieces), busily installing trunks, bags, and packing-cases in the suite engaged for the "great man of science" on the second floor of the east wing of the building. Neither the great man nor his companion was to be seen, however, both having retired to their rooms immediately upon their arrival—so Amédée informed me, as he wiped his brow after staggering up the steps under a load of books wrapped in sacking.

I made my evening ablutions removing a Joseph's coat of dust and paint; and came forth from my pavilion, hoping that Professor Keredec and his friend would not mind eating in the same garden with a man in a corduroy jacket and knickerbockers; but the gentlemen continued invisible to the public eye, and mine was the only table set for dinner in the garden. Up-stairs the curtains were carefully drawn across all the windows of the east wing; little leaks of orange, here and there, betraying the lights within. Glouglou, bearing a tray of covered dishes, was just entering the salon of the "Grande Suite," and the door closed quickly after him.

"It is to be supposed that Professor Keredec and

his friend are fatigued with their journey from Paris?" I began, a little later.

"Monsieur, they did not seem fatigued," said Amédée.

"But they dine in their own rooms to-night."

"Every night, monsieur. It is the order of Professor Keredec. And with their own valet-de-chambre to serve them. Eh?" He poured my coffee solemnly. "That is mysterious, to say the least, isn't it?"

"To say the very least," I agreed.

"Monsieur the professor is a man of secrets, it appears," continued Amédée. "When he wrote to Madame Brossard engaging his rooms, he instructed her to be careful that none of us should mention even his name; and to-day when he came, he spoke of his anxiety on that point."

"But you did mention it."

"To whom, monsieur?" asked the old fellow blankly.

"To me."

"But I told him I had not," said Amédée placidly. "It is the same thing."

"I wonder," I began, struck by a sudden thought, "if it will prove quite the same thing in my own case. I suppose you have not mentioned the circumstance of my being here to your friend, Jean Ferret of Quesnay?"

He looked at me reproachfully. "Has monsieur been troubled by the people of the château?"

" 'Troubled' by them?"

"Have they come to seek out monsieur and disturb him? Have they done anything whatever to show that they have heard monsieur is here?"

"No, certainly they haven't," I was obliged to retract at once. "I beg your pardon, Amédée."

"Ah, monsieur!" He made a deprecatory bow (which plunged me still deeper in shame), struck a match, and offered a light for my cigar with a forgiving hand. "All the same," he pursued, "it seems very mysterious—this Keredec affair!"

"To comprehend a great man, Amédée," I said, "is the next thing to sharing his greatness."

He blinked slightly, pondered a moment upon this sententious drivel, then very properly ignored it, reverting to his puzzle.

"But is it not incomprehensible that people should eat indoors this fine weather?"

I admitted that it was. I knew very well how hot and stuffy the salon of Madame Brossard's

"Grande Suite" must be, while the garden was
fragrant in the warm, dry night, and the outdoor
air like a gentle tonic. Nevertheless, Professor
Keredec and his friend preferred the salon.

When a man is leading a very quiet and isolated
life, it is inconceivable what trifles will occupy and
concentrate his attention. The smaller the com-
munity the more blowzy with gossip you are sure
to find it; and I have little doubt that when Friday
learned enough English, one of the first things Crusoe
did was to tell him some scandal about the goat.
Thus, though I treated the "Keredec affair" with
a seeming airiness to Amédée, I cunningly drew
the faithful rascal out, and fed my curiosity upon
his own (which, as time went on and the mystery
deepened, seemed likely to burst him), until, virtually, I was receiving, every evening at dinner, a
detailed report of the day's doings of Professor
Keredec and his companion.

The reports were voluminous, the details few.
The two gentlemen, as Amédée would relate, spent
their forenoons over books and writing in their
rooms. Professor Keredec's voice could often be
heard in every part of the inn; at times holding

forth with such protracted vehemence that only one explanation would suffice: the learned man was delivering a lecture to his companion.

"Say then!" exclaimed Amédée—"what king of madness is that? To make orations for only one auditor!"

He brushed away my suggestion that the auditor might be a stenographer to whom the professor was dictating chapters for a new book. The relation between the two men, he contended, was more like that between teacher and pupil. "But a pupil with gray hair!" he finished, raising his fat hands to heaven. "For that other monsieur has hair as gray as mine."

"That other monsieur" was farther described as a thin man, handsome, but with a "singular air," nor could my colleague more satisfactorily define this air, though he made a racking struggle to do so.

"In what does the peculiarity of his manner lie?" I asked.

"But it is not so much that his manner is peculiar, monsieur; it is an air about him that is singular. Truly!"

"But how is it singular?"

"Monsieur, it is very, very singular."

"You do not understand," I insisted. "What kind of singularity has the air of 'that other monsieur'?"

"It has," replied Amédée, with a powerful effort, "a very singular singularity."

This was as near as he could come, and, fearful of injuring him, I abandoned that phase of our subject.

The valet-de-chambre whom my fellow-lodgers had brought with them from Paris contributed nothing to the inn's knowledge of his masters, I learned. This struck me not only as odd, but unique, for French servants tell one another everything, and more—very much more. "But this is a silent man," said Amédée impressively. "Oh! very silent! He shakes his head wisely, yet he will not open his mouth. However, that may be because"—and now the explanation came—"because he was engaged only last week and knows nothing. Also, he is but temporary; he returns to Paris soon and Glouglou is to serve them."

I ascertained that although "that other monsieur" had gray hair, he was by no means a person of great age; indeed, Glouglou, who had seen him oftener than any other of the staff, maintained that he was quite young. Amédée's own opportunities for observation had been limited. Every afternoon the two gentlemen went for a walk; but they always came down from the gallery so quickly, he declared, and, leaving the inn by a rear entrance, plunged so hastily into the nearest by-path leading to the forest, that he caught little more than glimpses of them. They returned after an hour or so, entering the inn with the same appearance of haste to be out of sight, the professor always talking, "with the manner of an orator, but in English." Nevertheless, Amédée remarked, it was certain that Professor Keredec's friend was neither an American nor an Englishman.

"Why is it certain?" I asked.

"Monsieur, he drinks nothing but water, he does not smoke, and Glouglou says he speaks very pure French."

"Glouglou is an authority who resolves the difficulty. 'That other monsieur' is a Frenchman."

"But, monsieur, he is smooth-shaven."

"Perhaps he has been a maître d'hôtel."

"Eh! I wish one that _I_ know could hope to dress as well when he retires! Besides, Glouglou says that other monsieur eats his soup silently."

"I can find no flaw in the deduction," I said, rising to go to bed. "We must leave it there for to-night."

The next evening Amédée allowed me to perceive that he was concealing something under his arm as he stoked the coffee-machine, and upon my asking what it was, he glanced round the courtyard with histrionic slyness, placed the object on the table beside my cap, and stepped back to watch the impression, his manner that of one who declaims: "At last the missing papers are before you!"

"What is that?" I said.

"It is a book."

"I am persuaded by your candour, Amédée, as well as by the general appearance of this article," I returned as I picked it up, "that you are speaking the truth. But why do you bring it to me?"

"Monsieur," he replied, in the tones of an old conspirator, "this afternoon the professor and that other monsieur went as usual to walk in the forest." He bent over me, pretending to be busy with the coffee-machine, and lowering his voice to a hoarse whisper. "When they returned, this book fell from the pocket of that other moniseur's coat as he

ascended the stair, and he did not notice. Later
I shall return it by Glouglou, but I thought it wise
that monsieur should see it for himself."

The book was Wentworth's Algebra—elementary
principles. Painful recollections of my boyhood and
the binomial theorem rose in my mind as I let the
leaves turn under my fingers. "What do you make
of it?" I asked.

His tone became even more confidential. "Part
of it, monsieur, is in English; that is plain. I have
found an English word in it that I know—the
word 'O.' But much of the printing is also in
Arabic."

"Arabic!" I exclaimed.

"Yes, monsieur, look there." He laid a fat fore-
finger on "$(a + b)^2 = a^2 + 2ab + b^2$." "That is
Arabic. Old Gaston has been to Algeria, and he
says that he knows Arabic as well as he does French.
He looked at the book and told me it was Arabic.
Truly! Truly!"

"Did he translate any of it for you?"

"No, monsieur; his eyes pained him this afternoon. He says he will read it to-morrow."

"But you must return the book to-night."

"That is true. Eh! It leaves the mystery deeper

than ever, unless monsieur can find some clue in those parts of the book that are English."

I shed no light upon him. The book had been Greek to me in my tender years; it was a pleasure now to leave a fellow-being under the impression that it was Arabic.

But the volume took its little revenge upon me, for it increased my curiosity about Professor Keredec and "that other monsieur." Why were two grown men—one an eminent psychologist and the other a gray-haired youth with a singular air—carrying about on their walks a text-book for the instruction of boys of thirteen or fourteen?

The next day that curiosity of mine was piqued in earnest. It rained and I did not leave the inn, but sat under the great archway and took notes in colour of the shining road, bright drenched fields, and dripping sky. My back was toward the court-yard, that is, "three-quarters" to it, and about noon I became distracted from my work by a strong self-consciousness which came upon me without any visible or audible cause. Obeying an impulse, I swung round on my camp-stool and looked up directly at the gallery window of the salon of the "Grande Suite."

A man with a great white beard was standing at the window, half hidden by the curtain, watching me intently.

He perceived that I saw him and dropped the curtain immediately, a speck of colour in his buttonhole catching my eye as it fell.

The spy was Professor Keredec.

But why should he study me so slyly and yet so obviously? I had no intention of intruding upon him. Nor was I a psychological "specimen," though I began to suspect that "that other monsieur" *was*.

CHAPTER V

I HAD been painting in various parts of the forest, studying the early morning along the eastern fringe and moving deeper in as the day advanced. For the stillness and warmth of noon I went to the very woodland heart, and in the late afternoon moved westward to a glade—a chance arena open to the sky, the scene of my most audacious endeavours, for here I was trying to paint foliage luminous under those long shafts of sunshine which grow thinner but ruddier toward sunset. A path closely bordered by underbrush wound its way to the glade, crossed it, then wandered away into shady dingles again; and with my easel pitched in the mouth of this path, I sat at work, one late afternoon, wonderful for its still loveliness.

The path debouched abruptly on the glade and was so narrow that when I leaned back my elbows were in the bushes, and it needed care to keep my palette from being smirched by the leaves; though there was more room for my canvas and easel, as I had placed them at arm's length before me, fairly in the open.

I had the ambition to paint a picture here—to do the whole thing in the woods from day to day, instead of taking notes for the studio—and was at work upon a very foolish experiment: I had thought to render the light—broken by the branches and foliage—with broken brush-work, a short stroke of the kind that stung an elder painter to swear that its practitioners painted in shaking fear of the concierge appearing for the studio rent. The attempt was alluring, but when I rose from my camp-stool and stepped back into the path to get more distance for my canvas, I saw what a mess I was making of it. At the same time, my hand, falling into the capacious pocket of my jacket, encountered a package, my lunch, which I had forgotten to eat, whereupon, becoming suddenly aware that I was very hungry, I began to eat Amédée's good sandwiches without moving from where I stood.

Absorbed, gazing with abysmal disgust at my canvas, I was eating absent-mindedly—and with all the restraint and dignity of a Georgia darky attacking a watermelon—when a pleasant voice spoke from just behind me.

"Pardon, monsieur; permit me to pass, if you please."

That was all it said, very quietly and in French, but a gunshot might have startled me less.

I turned in confusion to behold a dark-eyed lady, charmingly dressed in lilac and white, waiting for me to make way so that she could pass.

Nay, let me leave no detail of my mortification unrecorded: I have just said that I "turned in confusion"; the truth is that I jumped like a kangaroo, but with infinitely less grace. And in my nervous haste to clear her way, meaning only to push the camp-stool out of the path with my foot, I put too much valour into the push, and with horror saw the camp-stool rise in the air and drop to the ground again nearly a third of the distance across the glade.

Upon that I squeezed myself back into the bushes, my ears singing and my cheeks burning.

There are women who will meet or pass a strange man in the woods or fields with as finished an air of being unaware of him (particularly if he be a rather shabby painter no longer young) as if the encounter took place on a city sidewalk; but this woman was not of that priggish kind. Her straightforward glance recognised my existence as a fellow-being; and she further acknowledged it by a faint smile, which was of courtesy only, however, and admitted no ref-

erence to the fact that at the first sound of her voice
I had leaped into the air, kicked a camp-stool twenty
feet, and now stood blushing, so shamefully stuffed
with sandwich that I dared not speak.

"Thank you," she said as she went by; and made
me a little bow so graceful that it almost consoled
me for my caperings.

I stood looking after her as she crossed the clearing and entered the cool winding of the path on the
other side.

I stared and wished—wished that I could have
painted her into my picture, with the thin, ruddy
sunshine flecking her dress; wished that I had not
cut such an idiotic figure. I stared until her filmy
summer hat, which was the last bit of her to disappear, had vanished. Then, discovering that I still
held the horrid remains of a sausage-sandwich in my
hand, I threw it into the underbrush with unnecessary
force, and, recovering my camp-stool, sat down to
work again.

I did not immediately begin.

The passing of a pretty woman anywhere never
comes to be quite of no moment to a man, and the
passing of a pretty woman in the greenwood is an
episode—even to a middle-aged landscape painter.

"An episode?" quoth I. I should be ashamed to with-
hold the truth out of my fear to be taken for a senti-
mentalist: this woman who had passed was of great
and instant charm; it was as if I had heard a serenade
there in the woods—and at thought of the jig I had
danced to it my face burned again.

With a sigh of no meaning, I got my eyes down to
my canvas and began to peck at it perfunctorily,
when a snapping of twigs underfoot and a swishing
of branches in the thicket warned me of a second
intruder, not approaching by the path, but forcing
a way toward it through the underbrush, and very
briskly too, judging by the sounds.

He burst out into the glade a few paces from me,
a tall man in white flannels, liberally decorated with
brambles and clinging shreds of underbrush. A
streamer of vine had caught about his shoulders;
there were leaves on his bare head, and this, together
with the youthful sprightliness of his light figure
and the naive activity of his approach, gave me a
very faunlike first impression of him.

At sight of me he stopped short.

"Have you seen a lady in a white and lilac dress
and with roses in her hat?" he demanded, omitting
all preface and speaking with a quick eagerness

which caused me no wonder—for I had seen the lady.

What did surprise me, however, was the instantaneous certainty with which I recognised the speaker from Amédée's description; certainty founded on the very item which had so dangerously strained the old fellow's powers.

My sudden gentleman was strikingly good-looking, his complexion so clear and boyishly healthy, that, except for his gray hair, he might have passed for twenty-two or twenty-three, and even as it was I guessed his years short of thirty; but there are plenty of handsome young fellows with prematurely gray hair, and, as Amédée said, though out of the world we were near it. It was the new-comer's "singular air" which established his identity. Amédée's vagueness had irked me, but the thing itself—the "singular air"—was not at all vague. Instantly perceptible, it was an investiture; marked, definite—and intangible. My interrogator was "that other monsieur."

In response to his question I asked him another: "Were the roses real or artificial?"

"I don't know," he answered, with what I took to be a whimsical assumption of gravity. "It wouldn't matter, would it? Have you seen her?"

He stooped to brush the brambles from his trousers, sending me a sidelong glance from his blue eyes, which were brightly confident and inquiring, like a boy's. At the same time it struck me that whatever the nature of the singularity investing him it partook of nothing repellent, but, on the contrary, measurably enhanced his attractiveness; making him "different" and lending him a distinction which, without it, he might have lacked. And yet, patent as this singularity must have been to the dullest, it was something quite apart from any eccentricity of manner, though, heaven knows, I was soon to think him odd enough.

"Isn't your description," I said gravely, thinking to suit my humour to his own, "somewhat too general? Over yonder a few miles lies Houlgate. Trouville itself is not so far, and this is the season. A great many white hats trimmed with roses might come for a stroll in these woods. If you would complete the items—" and I waved my hand as if inviting him to continue.

"I have seen her only once before," he responded promptly, with a seriousness apparently quite genuine. "That was from my window at an inn, three days ago. She drove by in an open carriage without looking up, but I could see that she was very handsome. No—" he broke off abruptly, but as quickly resumed—"handsome isn't just what I mean. Lovely, I should say. That is more like her and a better thing to be, shouldn't you think so?"

"Probably—yes—I think so," I stammered, in considerable amazement.

"She went by quickly," he said, as if he were talking in the most natural and ordinary way in the world, "but I noticed that while she was in the shade of the inn her hair appeared to be dark, though when the carriage got into the sunlight again it looked fair."

I had noticed the same thing when the lady who had passed emerged from the shadows of the path into the sunshine of the glade, but I did not speak of it now; partly because he gave me no opportunity, partly because I was almost too astonished to speak at all, for I was no longer under the delusion that he had any humourous or whimsical intention.

"A little while ago," he went on, "I was up in the branches of a tree over yonder, and I caught a glimpse of a lady in a light dress and a white hat and I thought it might be the same. She wore a dress like that and a white hat with roses when she drove by the inn. I am very anxious to see her again."

"You seem to be!"

"And haven't you seen her? Hasn't she passed this way?"

He urged the question with the same strange eagerness which had marked his manner from the first, a manner which confounded me by its absurd resemblance to that of a boy who had not mixed with other boys and had never been teased. And yet his expression was intelligent and alert; nor was there anything abnormal or "queer" in his good-humoured gaze.

"I think that I may have seen her," I began slowly; "but if you do not know her I should not advise——"

I was interrupted by a shout and the sound of a large body plunging in the thicket. At this the face of "that other monsieur" flushed slightly; he smiled, but seemed troubled.

"That is a friend of mine," he said. "I am afraid he will want me to go back with him." And he raised an answering shout.

Professor Keredec floundered out through the last row of saplings and bushes, his beard embellished with a broken twig, his big face red and perspiring. He was a fine, a mighty man, ponderous of shoulder, monumental of height, stupendous of girth; there was cloth enough in the hot-looking black frock-coat he wore for the canopy of a small pavilion. Half a dozen books were under his arm, and in his hand he carried a hat which evidently belonged to "that other monsieur," for his own was on his head.

One glance of scrutiny and recognition he shot at me from his silver-rimmed spectacles; and seized the young man by the arm.

"Ha, my friend!" he exclaimed in a bass voice of astounding power and depth, "that is one way to study botany: to jump out of the middle of a high tree and to run like a crazy man!" He spoke with a strong accent and a thunderous rolling of the "r." "What was I to think?" he demanded. "What has arrived to you?"

"I saw a lady I wished to follow," the other answered promptly.

"A lady! What lady?"

"The lady who passed the inn three days ago. I spoke of her then, you remember."

"*Tonnerre de Dieu!*" Keredec slapped his thigh with the sudden violence of a man who remembers that he has forgotten something, and as a final addition to my amazement, his voice rang more of remorse than of reproach. "Have I never told you that to follow strange ladies is one of the things you cannot do?"

"That other monsieur" shook his head. "No, you have never told me that. I do not understand it," he said, adding irrelevantly, "I believe this gentleman knows her. He says he thinks he has seen her."

"If you please, we must not trouble this gentleman about it," said the professor hastily. "Put on your hat, in the name of a thousand saints, and let us go!"

"But I wish to ask him her name," urged the other, with something curiously like the obstinacy of a child. "I wish——"

"No, no!" Keredec took him by the arm. "We must go. We shall be late for our dinner."

"But why?" persisted the young man.

"Not now!" The professor removed his broad felt hat and hurriedly wiped his vast and steaming brow —a magnificent structure, corniced, at this moment, with anxiety. "It is better if we do not discuss it now."

"But I might not meet him again."

Professor Keredec turned toward me with a half-desperate, half-apologetic laugh which was like the rumbling of heavy wagons over a block pavement; and in his flustered face I thought I read a signal of genuine distress.

"I do not know the lady," I said with some sharpness. "I have never seen her until this afternoon."

Upon this "that other monsieur" astonished me in good earnest. Searching my eyes eagerly with his clear, inquisitive gaze, he took a step toward me and said:

"You are sure you are telling the truth?"

The professor uttered an exclamation of horror, sprang forward, and clutched his friend's arm again. "*Malheureux!*" he cried, and then to me: "Sir, you will give him pardon if you can? He has no meaning to be rude."

"Rude?" The young man's voice showed both astonishment and pain. "Was that rude? I didn't know. I didn't mean to be rude, God knows! Ah," he said sadly, "I do nothing but make mistakes. I hope you will forgive me."

He lifted his hand as if in appeal, and let it drop to his side; and in the action, as well as in the tone of his voice and his attitude of contrition, there was something that reached me suddenly, with the touch of pathos.

"Never mind," I said. "I am only sorry that it was the truth."

"Thank you," he said, and turned humbly to Keredec.

"Ha, that is better!" shouted the great man, apparently relieved of a vast weight. "We shall go home now and eat a good dinner. But first—" his silver-rimmed spectacles twinkled upon me, and he bent his Brobdingnagian back in a bow which against my will reminded me of the curtseys performed by Orloff's dancing bears—"first let me speak some words for myself. My dear sir"—he addressed himself to me with grave formality—"do not suppose I have no realization that other excuses should be made to you. Believe me, they shall be. It is now that I see it is fortunate for us that you are our fellow-innsman at *Les Trois Pigeons*."

I was unable to resist the opportunity, and, affecting considerable surprise, interrupted him with the apparently guileless query:

"Why, how did you know that?"

Professor Keredec's laughter rumbled again, growing deeper and louder till it reverberated in the woods and a hundred hale old trees laughed back at him.

"Ho, ho, ho!" he shouted. "But you shall not take me for a window-curtain spy! That is a fine reputation I give myself with you! Ho, ho!"

Then, followed submissively by "that other monsieur," he strode into the path and went thundering forth through the forest.

CHAPTER VI

NO doubt the most absurd thing I could have done after the departure of Professor Keredec and his singular friend would have been to settle myself before my canvas again with the intention of painting—and that is what I did. At least, I resumed my camp-stool and went through some of the motions habitually connected with the act of painting.

I remember that the first time in my juvenile reading I came upon the phrase, "seated in a brown study," I pictured my hero in a brown chair, beside a brown table, in a room hung with brown paper. Later, being enlightened, I was ambitious to display the figure myself, but the uses of ordinary correspondence allowed the occasion for it to remain unoffered. Let me not only seize upon the present opportunity but gild it, for the adventure of the afternoon left me in a study which was, at its mildest, a profound purple.

The confession has been made of my curiosity concerning my fellow-lodgers at *Les Trois Pigeons;*

however, it had been comparatively a torpid growth; my meeting with them served to enlarge it so suddenly and to such proportions that I wonder it did not strangle me. In fine, I sat there brush-paddling my failure like an automaton, and saying over and over aloud, "What is wrong with him? What *is* wrong with him?"

This was the sillier inasmuch as the word "wrong" (bearing any significance of a darkened mind) had not the slightest application to "that other monsieur." There had been neither darkness nor dullness; his eyes, his expression, his manner, betrayed no hint of wildness; rather they bespoke a quick and amiable intelligence—the more amazing that he had shown himself ignorant of things a child of ten would know. Amédée and his fellows of *Les Trois Pigeons* had judged wrongly of his nationality; his face was of the lean, right, American structure; but they had hit the relation between the two men: Keredec was the master and "that other monsieur" the scholar— a pupil studying boys' textbooks and receiving instruction in matters and manners that children are taught. And yet I could not believe him to be a simple case of arrested development. For the matter of that, I did not like to think of him as a "case"

at all. There had been something about his bright
youthfulness—perhaps it was his quick contrition for
his rudeness, perhaps it was a certain wistful quality
he had, perhaps it was his very "singularity"—
which appealed as directly to my liking as it did
urgently to my sympathy.

I came out of my vari-coloured study with a start,
caused by the discovery that I had absent-mindedly
squeezed upon my palette the entire contents of an
expensive tube of cobalt violet, for which I had no
present use; and sighing (for, of necessity, I am an
economical man), I postponed both of my problems
till another day, determined to efface the one with
a palette knife and a rag soaked in turpentine, and
to defer the other until I should know more of my
fellow-lodgers at Madame Brossard's.

The turpentine rag at least proved effective; I
scoured away the last tokens of my failure with it,
wishing that life were like the canvas and that men
had knowledge of the right celestial turpentine.
After that I cleaned my brushes, packed and shoul-
dered my kit, and, with a final imprecation upon all
sausage-sandwiches, took up my way once more to
Les Trois Pigeons.

Presently I came upon an intersecting path where,

on my previous excursions, I had always borne to the right; but this evening, thinking to discover a shorter cut, I went straight ahead. Striding along at a good gait and chanting sonorously, "On Linden when the sun was low," I left the rougher boscages of the forest behind me and emerged, just at sunset, upon an orderly fringe of woodland where the ground was neat and unencumbered, and the trimmed trees stood at polite distances, bowing slightly to one another with small, well-bred rustlings.

The light was somewhere between gold and pink when I came into this lady's boudoir of a grove. "Isar flowing rapidly" ceased its tumult abruptly, and Linden saw no sterner sight that evening: my voice and my feet stopped simultaneously—for I stood upon Quesnay ground.

Before me stretched a short broad avenue of turf, leading to the château gates. These stood open, a gravelled driveway climbing thence by easy stages between kempt shrubberies to the crest of the hill, where the gray roof and red chimney-pots of the château were glimpsed among the tree-tops. The slope was terraced with strips of flower-gardens and intervals of sward; and against the green of a rising lawn I marked the figure of a woman, pausing to bend over some flowering bush. The figure was too slender to be mistaken for that of the present chatelaine of Quesnay: in Miss Elizabeth's regal amplitude there was never any hint of fragility. The lady upon the slope, then, I concluded, must be Madame d'Armand, the inspiration of Amédée's "Monsieur has much to live for!"

Once more this day I indorsed that worthy man's opinion, for, though I was too far distant to see clearly, I knew that roses trimmed Madame d'Armand's white hat, and that she had passed me, no long time since, in the forest.

I took off my cap.

"I have the honour to salute you," I said aloud. "I make my apologies for misbehaving with sandwiches and camp-stools in your presence, Madame d'Armand."

Something in my own pronunciation of her name struck me as reminiscent: save for the prefix, it had sounded like "Harman," as a Frenchman might pronounce it.

Foreign names involve the French in terrible difficulties. Hughes, an English friend of mine, has lived in France some five-and-thirty years without reconciling himself to being known as "Monsieur Ig."

"Armand" might easily be Jean Ferret's translation of "Harman." Had he and Amédée in their admiration conferred the prefix because they considered it a plausible accompaniment to the lady's gentle bearing? It was not impossible; it was, I concluded, very probable.

I had come far out of my way, so I retraced my steps to the intersection of the paths, and thence made for the inn by my accustomed route. The light failed under the roofing of foliage long before I was free of the woods, and I emerged upon the road to *Les Trois Pigeons* when twilight had turned to dusk.

Not far along the road from where I came into it, stood an old, brown, deep-thatched cottage—a branch of brushwood over the door prettily beckoning travellers to the knowledge that cider was here for the thirsty; and as I drew near I perceived that one availed himself of the invitation. A group stood about the open door, the lamp-light from within disclosing the head of the house filling a cup for the wayfarer; while honest Mère Baudry and two generations of younger Baudrys clustered to miss no word of the interchange of courtesies between Père Baudry and his chance patron.

It afforded me some surprise to observe that the latter was a most mundane and elaborate wayfarer, indeed; a small young man very lightly made, like a jockey, and point-device in khaki, puttees, pongee cap, white-and-green stock, a knapsack on his back, and a bamboo stick under his arm; altogether equipped to such a high point of pedestrianism that a cynical person might have been reminded of loud calls for wine at some hostelry in the land of opera bouffe. He was speaking fluently, though with a detestable accent, in a rough-and-ready, pick-up dialect of Parisian slang, evidently under the pleasant delusion that he employed the French language, while Père Baudry contributed his share of the conversation in a slow patois. As both men spoke at the same time and neither understood two consecutive words the other said, it struck me that the dialogue might prove unproductive of any highly important results this side of Michaelmas; therefore, discovering that the very pedestrian gentleman was making some sort of inquiry concerning *Les Trois Pigeons*, I came to a halt and proffered aid.

"Are you looking for Madame Brossard's?" I asked in English.

The traveller uttered an exclamation and faced

about with a jump, birdlike for quickness. He did not reply to my question with the same promptness; however, his deliberation denoted scrutiny, not sloth. He stood peering at me sharply until I repeated it. Even then he protracted his examination of me, a favour I was unable to return with any interest, owing to the circumstance of his back being toward the light. Nevertheless, I got a clear enough impression of his alert, well-poised little figure, and of a hatchety little face, and a pair of shrewd little eyes, which (I thought) held a fine little conceit of his whole little person. It was a type of fellow-countryman not altogether unknown about certain "American Bars" of Paris, and usually connected (more or less directly) with what is known to the people of France as "le Sport."

"Say," he responded in a voice of unpleasant nasality, finally deciding upon speech, "you're 'Nummeric'n, ain't you?"

"Yes," I returned. "I thought I heard you inquiring for——"

"Well, m' friend, you can sting me!" he interrupted with condescending jocularity. "My style French does f'r them camels up in Paris all right. *Me* at Nice, Monte Carlo, Chantilly—bow to the p'fess'r; he's *right!* But down here I don't seem to be *gud* enough f'r these sheep-dogs; anyway they bark different. I'm lukkin' fer a hotel called *Les Trois Pigeons.*"

"I am going there," I said; "I will show you the way."

"Whur is 't?" he asked, not moving.

I pointed to the lights of the inn, flickering across the fields. "Yonder—beyond the second turn of the road," I said, and, as he showed no signs of accompanying me, I added, "I am rather late."

"Oh, I ain't goin' there t'night. It's too dark t' see anything now," he remarked, to my astonishment. "Dives and the choo-choo back t' little ole Trouville f'r mine! I on'y wanted to take a *luk* at this pigeon-house joint."

"Do you mind my inquiring," I said, "what you expected to see at *Les Trois Pigeons?*"

"Why!" he exclaimed, as if astonished at the question, "I'm a tourist. Makin' a pedestrun trip t' all the reg'ler sights." And, inspired to eloquence, he added, as an afterthought: "As it were."

"A tourist?" I echoed, with perfect incredulity.

"That's whut I am, m' friend," he returned firmly. "You don't have to have a red dope-book in one hand and a thoid-class choo-choo ticket in the other to be a tourist, do you?"

"But if you will pardon me," I said, "where did you get the notion that *Les Trois Pigeons* is one of the regular sights?"

"Ain't it in all the books?"

"I don't think that it is mentioned in any of the guide-books."

"*No!* I didn't say it *was*, m' friend," he retorted with contemptuous pity. "I mean them history-books. It's in all o' *them!*"

"This is strange news," said I. "I should be very much interested to read them!"

"Lookahere," he said, taking a step nearer me; "in oinest now, on your woid: Didn' more'n half them Jeanne d'Arc tamales live at that hotel wunst?"

"Nobody of historical importance—or any other kind of importance, so far as I know—ever lived there," I informed him. "The older portions of the inn once belonged to an ancient farm-house, that is all."

"On the level," he demanded, "didn't that William the Conker nor *none* o' them ancient gilt-edges live there?"

"No."

"Stung again!" He broke into a sudden loud

cackle of laughter. "Why! the feller tole me 'at this here Pigeon place was all three rings when it come t' history. Yessir! Tall, thin feller he was, in a three-button cutaway, English make, and kind of red-complected, with a sandy *mus*-tache," pursued the pedestrian, apparently fearing his narrative might lack colour. "I met him right comin' out o' the Casino at Trouville, yes'day aft'noon; c'udn' a' b'en more'n four o'clock—hol' on though, yes 'twas, 'twas nearer five, about twunty minutes t' five, say —an' this feller tells me—" He cackled with laughter as palpably disingenuous as the corroborative details he thought necessary to muster; then he became serious, as if marvelling at his own wondrous verdancy. "M' friend, that feller soitn'y found me easy. But he can't say I ain't game; he passes me the limes, but I'm jest man enough to drink his health fer it in this sweet, sound ole-fashioned cider 'at ain't got a headache in a barrel of it. He played me *gud*, and here's *to* him!"

Despite the heartiness of the sentiment, my honest tourist's enthusiasm seemed largely histrionic, and his quaffing of the beaker too reminiscent of drain-the-wine-cup-free in the second row of the chorus, for he absently allowed it to dangle from his hand

before raising it to his lips. However, not all of its
contents was spilled, and he swallowed a mouthful
of the sweet, sound, old-fashioned cider—but by
mistake, I was led to suppose, from the expression of
displeasure which became so deeply marked upon
his countenance as to be noticeable, even in the
feeble lamplight.

I tarried no longer, but bidding this good youth
and the generations of Baudry good-night, hastened
on to my belated dinner.

"Amédée," I said, when my cigar was lighted and
the usual hour of consultation had arrived; "isn't
that old lock on the chest where Madame Brossard
keeps her silver getting rather rusty?"

"Monsieur, we have no thieves here. We are out
of the world."

"Yes, but Trouville is not so far away."

"Truly."

"Many strange people go to Trouville: grand-
dukes, millionaires, opera singers, princes, jockeys,
gamblers——"

"Truly, truly!"

"And tourists," I finished.

"That is well known," assented Amédée, nodding.

"It follows," I continued with the impressiveness

of all logicians, "that many strange people may come
from Trouville.   In their excursions to the surround-
ing points of interest——"

"Eh, monsieur, but that is true!" he interrupted,
laying his right forefinger across the bridge of his
nose, which was his gesture when he remembered anything suddenly.   "There was a strange monsieur
from Trouville here this very day."

"What kind of person was he?"

"A foreigner, but I could not tell from what
country."

"What time of day was he here?" I asked, with
growing interest.

"Toward the middle of the afternoon. I was alone,
except for Glouglou, when he came. He wished to
see the whole house and I showed him what I could,
except of course monsieur's pavilion, and the Grande
Suite. Monsieur the Professor and that other monsieur had gone to the forest, but I did not feel at
liberty to exhibit their rooms without Madame Brossard's permission, and she was spending the day at
Dives. Besides," added the good man, languidly
snapping a napkin at a moth near one of the
candles, "the doors were locked."

"This person was a tourist?" I asked, after a

pause during which Amédée seemed peacefully unaware of the rather concentrated gaze I had fixed
upon him.

"Of a kind. In speaking he employed many
peculiar expressions, more like a thief of a Parisian
cabman than of the polite world."

"The devil he did!" said I. "Did he tell you why
he wished to see the whole house? Did he contemplate taking rooms here?"

"No, monsieur, it appears that his interest was
historical. At first I should not have taken him for a
man of learning, yet he gave me a great piece of
information; a thing quite new to me, though I have
lived here so many years. We are distinguished in
history, it seems, and at one time both William the
Conqueror and that brave Jeanne d'Arc——"

I interrupted sharply, dropping my cigar and
leaning across the table:

"How was this person dressed?"

"Monsieur, he was very much the pedestrian."

And so, for that evening, we had something to
talk about besides "that other monsieur"; indeed,
we found our subject so absorbing that I forgot
to ask Amédée whether it was he or Jean Ferret
who had prefixed the "de" to "Armand."

CHAPTER VII

THE cat that fell from the top of the Washington monument, and scampered off unhurt was killed by a dog at the next corner. Thus a certain painter-man, winged with canvases and easel, might have been seen to depart hurriedly from a poppy-sprinkled field, an infuriated Norman stallion in close attendance, and to fly safely over a stone wall of good height, only to turn his ankle upon an unconsidered pebble, some ten paces farther on; the nose of the stallion projected over the wall, snorting joy thereat. The ankle was one which had turned aforetime; it was an old weakness: moreover, it was mine. I was the painter-man.

I could count on little less than a week of idleness within the confines of *Les Trois Pigeons;* and reclining among cushions in a wicker long-chair looking out from my pavilion upon the drowsy garden on a hot noontide, I did not much care. It was cooler indoors, comfortable enough; the open door framed the courtyard where pigeons were

strutting on the gravel walks between flower-beds.
Beyond, and thrown deeper into the perspective
by the outer frame of the great archway, road and
fields and forest fringes were revealed, lying tremulously in the hot sunshine. The foreground gained
a human (though not lively) interest from the
ample figure of our *maître d'hôtel* reposing in a
rustic chair which had enjoyed the shade of an
arbour about an hour earlier, when first occupied,
but now stood in the broiling sun. At times Amédée's
upper eyelids lifted as much as the sixteenth of an
inch, and he made a hazy gesture as if to wave the
sun away, or, when the table-cloth upon his left
arm slid slowly earthward, he adjusted it with a
petulant jerk, without material interruption to his
siesta. Meanwhile Glouglou, rolling and smoking
cigarettes in the shade of a clump of lilac, watched
with button eyes the noddings of his superior,
and, at the cost of some convulsive writhings,
constrained himself to silent laughter.

A heavy step crunched the gravel and I heard
my name pronounced in a deep inquiring rumble
—the voice of Professor Keredec, no less. Nor
was I greatly surprised, since our meeting in the
forest had led me to expect some advances on his

part toward friendliness, or, at least, in the direction of a better acquaintance. However, I withheld my reply for a moment to make sure I had heard aright.

The name was repeated.

"Here I am," I called, "in the pavilion, if you wish to see me."

"Aha! I hear you become an invalid, my dear sir." With that the professor's great bulk loomed in the doorway against the glare outside. "I have come to condole with you, if you allow it."

"To smoke with me, too, I hope," I said, not a little pleased.

"That I will do," he returned, and came in slowly, walking with perceptible lameness. "The sympathy I offer is genuine: it is not only from the heart, it is from the *latissimus dorsi*," he continued, seating himself with a cavernous groan. "I am your *confrère* in illness, my dear sir. I have choosed this fine weather for rheumatism of the back."

"I hope it is not painful."

"Ha, it is so-so," he rumbled, removing his spectacles and wiping his eyes, dazzled by the sun. "There is more of me than of most men—more to suffer. Nature was generous to the little germs when she made this big Keredec; she offered them room for their campaigns of war."

"You'll take a cigarette?"

"I thank you; if you do not mind, I smoke my pipe."

He took from his pocket a worn leather case, which he opened, disclosing a small, browned clay bowl of the kind workmen use; and, fitting it with a red stem, he filled it with a dark and sinister tobacco from a pouch. "Always my pipe for me," he said, and applied a match, inhaling the smoke as other men inhale the light smoke of cigarettes. "Ha, it is good! It is wicked for the insides, but it is good for the soul." And clouds wreathed his great beard like a storm on Mont Blanc as he concluded, with gusto, "It is my first pipe since yesterday."

"That is being a good smoker," I ventured sententiously; "to whet indulgence with abstinence."

"My dear sir," he protested, "I am a man without even enough virtue to be an epicure. When I am alone I am a chimney with no hebdomadary repose; I smoke forever. It is on account of my young friend I am temperate now."

"He has never smoked, your young friend?" I

asked, glancing at my visitor rather curiously, I fear.

"Mr. Saffren has no vices." Professor Keredec replaced his silver-rimmed spectacles and turned them upon me with serene benevolence. "He is in good condition, all pure, like little children— and so if I smoke near him he chokes and has water at the eyes, though he does not complain. Just now I take a vacation: it is his hour for study, but I think he looks more out of the front window than at his book. He looks very much from the window"—there was a muttering of subterranean thunder somewhere, which I was able to locate in the professor's torso, and took to be his expression of a chuckle—"yes, very much, since the passing of that charming lady some days ago."

"You say your young friend's name is Saffren?"

"Oliver Saffren." The benevolent gaze continued to rest upon me, but a shadow like a faint anxiety darkened the Homeric brow, and an odd notion entered my mind (without any good reason) that Professor Keredec was wondering what I thought of the name. I uttered some commonplace syllable of no moment, and there ensued a pause during which the seeming shadow upon my visitor's forehead became a reality, deepening to a look of perplexity and trouble.   Finally he said abruptly: "It is about him that I have come to talk to you."

"I shall be very glad," I murmured, but he brushed the callow formality aside with a gesture of remonstrance.

"Ha, my dear sir," he cried; "but you are a man of feeling! We are both old enough to deal with more than just these little words of the mouth! It was the way you have received my poor young gentleman's excuses when he was so rude, which make me wish to talk with you on such a subject; it is why I would not have you believe Mr. Saffren and me two very suspected individuals who hide here like two bad criminals!"

"No, no," I protested hastily. "The name of Professor Keredec——"

"The name of *no* man," he thundered, interrupting, "can protect his reputation when he is caught peeping from a curtain! Ha, my dear sir! I know what you think. You think, 'He is a nice fine man, that old professor, oh, very nice—only he hides behind the curtains sometimes! Very fine man, oh, yes; only he is a spy.' Eh? Ha, ha! That is what you have been thinking, my dear sir!"

"Not at all," I laughed; "I thought you might fear that *I* was a spy."

"Eh?" He became sharply serious upon the instant. "What made you think that?"

"I supposed you might be conducting some experiments, or perhaps writing a book which you wished to keep from the public for a time, and that possibly you might imagine that I was a reporter."

"So! And *that* is all," he returned, with evident relief. "No, my dear sir, I was the spy; it is the truth; and I was spying upon you. I confess my shame. I wish very much to know what you were like, what kind of a man you are. And so," he concluded with an opening of the hands, palms upward, as if to show that nothing remained for concealment, "and so I have watched you."

"Why?" I asked.

"The explanation is so simple: it was necessary."

"Because of—of Mr. Saffren?" I said slowly, and with some trepidation.

"Precisely." The professor exhaled a cloud of smoke. "Because I am sensitive for him, and because in a certain way I am—how should it be said?—perhaps it is near the truth to say, I am his guardian."

"I see."

"Forgive me," he rejoined quickly, "but I am afraid you do not see. I am not his guardian by the law."

"I had not supposed that you were," I said.

"Why not?"

"Because, though he puzzled me and I do not understand his case—his case, so to speak, I have not for a moment thought him insane."

"Ha, my dear sir, you are right!" exclaimed Keredec, beaming on me, much pleased. "You are a thousand times right; he is as sane as yourself or myself or as anybody in the whole wide world! Ha! he is now much *more* sane, for his mind is not yet confused and becobwebbed with the useless things you and I put into ours. It is open and clear like the little children's mind. And it is a good mind! It is only a little learning, a little experience, that he lacks. A few months more—ha, at the greatest, a year from now—and he will not be different any longer; he will be like the rest of us. Only"—the professor leaned forward and his big fist came down on the arm of his chair—"he shall be better than the rest of us! But if strange people were to see him now," he continued leaning back and dropping his voice to a more confidential tone, "it would not do. This poor world is full of fools; there are so many who judge quickly. If they should see him now, they might think he is not just right in his brain; and then, as it could happen so easily, those same people might meet him again after a while. 'Ha,' they would say, 'there was a time when that young man was insane. I knew him!' And so he might go through his life with those clouds over him. Those clouds are black clouds, they can make more harm than our old sins, and I wish to save my friend from them. So I have brought him here to this quiet place where nobody comes, and we can keep from meeting any foolish people. But, my dear sir"—he leaned forward again, and spoke emphatically—"it would be barbarous for men of intelligence to live in the same house and go always hiding from one another! Let us dine together this evening, if you will, and not only this evening but every evening you are willing to share with us and do not wish to be alone. It will be good for us. We are three men like hermits, far out of the world, but—a thousand saints!—let us be civilised to one another!"

"With all my heart," I said.

"Ha! I wish you to know my young man," Keredec went on. "You will like him—no man of feeling could keep himself from liking him—and he is your fellow-countryman. I hope you will be his friend. He should make friends, for he needs them."

"I think he has a host of them," said I, "in Professor Keredec."

My visitor looked at me quizzically for a moment, shook his head and sighed. "That is only one small man in a big body, that Professor Keredec. And yet," he went on sadly, "it is all the friends that poor boy has in this world. You will dine with us to-night?"

Acquiescing cheerfully, I added: "You will join me at the table on my veranda, won't you? I can hobble that far but not much farther."

Before answering he cast a sidelong glance at the arrangement of things outside the door. The screen of honeysuckle ran partly across the front of the little porch, about half of which it concealed from the garden and consequently from the road beyond the archway. I saw that he took note of this before he pointed to that corner of the veranda most closely screened by the vines and said:

"May the table be placed yonder?"

"Certainly; I often have it there, even when I am alone."

"Ha, that is good," he exclaimed. "It is not human for a Frenchman to eat in the house in good weather."

"It is a pity," I said, "that I should have been such a bugbear."

This remark was thoroughly disingenuous, for, although I did not doubt that anything he told me was perfectly true, nor that he had made as complete a revelation as he thought consistent with his duty toward the young man in his charge, I did not believe that his former precautions were altogether due to my presence at the inn.

And I was certain that while he might fear for his friend some chance repute of insanity, he had greater terrors than that. As to their nature I had no clew; nor was it my affair to be guessing; but whatever they were, the days of security at *Les Trois Pigeons* had somewhat eased Professor Keredec's mind in regard to them. At least, his anxiety was sufficiently assuaged to risk dining out of doors with only my screen of honeysuckle between his charge and curious eyes. So much was evident.

"The reproach is deserved," he returned, after a pause. "It is to be wished that all our bugbears might offer as pleasant a revelation, if we had the courage, or the slyness"—he laughed—"to investigate them."

I made a reply of similar gallantry and he got to his feet, rubbing his back as he rose.

"Ha, I am old! old! Rheumatism in warm weather: that is ugly. Now I must go to my boy and see what he can make of his Gibbon. The poor fellow! I think he finds the decay of Rome worse than rheumatism in summer!"

He replaced his pipe in its case, and promising heartily that it should not be the last he would smoke in my company and domain, was making slowly for the door when he paused at a sound from the road.

We heard the rapid hoof-beats of a mettled horse. He crossed our vision and the open archway: a high-stepping hackney going well, driven by a lady in a light trap which was half full of wild flowers. It was a quick picture, like a flash of the cinematograph, but the pose of the lady as a driver was seen to be of a commanding grace, and though she was not in white but in light blue, and her plain

sailor hat was certainly not trimmed with roses, I
had not the least difficulty in recognising her. At
the same instant there was a hurried clatter of footsteps upon the stairway leading from the gallery;
the startled pigeons fluttered up from the garden-
path, betaking themselves to flight, and "that other
monsieur" came leaping across the courtyard,
through the archway and into the road.

"Glouglou! Look quickly!" he called loudly, in
French, as he came; "Who is that lady?"

Glouglou would have replied, but the words were
taken out of his mouth. Amédée awoke with a
frantic start and launched himself at the archway,
carroming from its nearest corner and hurtling on-
ward at a speed which for once did not diminish
in proportion to his progress.

"That lady, monsieur?" he gasped, checking himself at the young man's side and gazing after the
trap, "that is Madame d'Armand."

"Madame d'Armand," Saffren repeated the name
slowly. "Her name is Madame d'Armand."

"Yes, monsieur," said Amédée complacently; "it
is an American lady who has married a French
nobleman."

CHAPTER VIII

LIKE most painters, I have supposed the tools of my craft harder to manipulate than those of others. The use of words, particularly, seemed readier, handier for the contrivance of effects than pigments. I thought the language of words less elusive than that of colour, leaving smaller margin for unintended effects; and, believing in complacent good faith that words conveyed exact meanings exactly, it was my innocent conception that almost anything might be so described in words that all who read must inevitably perceive that thing precisely. If this were true, there would be little work for the lawyers, who produce such tortured pages in the struggle to be definite, who swing riches from one family to another, save men from violent death or send them to it, and earn fortunes for themselves through the dangerous inadequacies of words. I have learned how great was my mistake, and now I am wishing I could shift paper for canvas, that I might paint the young man who came to interest me so deeply.

100

I wish I might present him here in colour instead
of trusting to this unstable business of words,
so wily and undependable, with their shimmering
values, that you cannot turn your back upon them
for two minutes but they will be shouting a hundred things which they were not meant to tell.

To make the best of necessity: what I have
written of him—my first impressions—must be taken
as the picture, although it be but a gossamer sketch
in the air, instead of definite work with well-ground
pigments to show forth a portrait, to make you
see flesh and blood. It must take the place of something contrived with my own tools to reveal what
the following days revealed him to me, and what
it was about him (evasive of description) which made
me so soon, as Keredec wished, his friend.

Life among our kin and kind is made pleasanter
by our daily platitudes. Who is more tedious than
the man incessantly struggling to avoid the banal?
Nature rules that such a one will produce nothing
better than epigram and paradox, saying old, old
things in a new way, or merely shifting object for
subject—and his wife's face, when he shines for a
circle, is worth a glance. With no further apology,
I declare that I am a person who has felt few posi-

tive likes or dislikes for people in this life, and I
did deeply like my fellow-lodgers at *Les Trois
Pigeons*. Liking for both men increased with acquaintance, and for the younger I came to feel,
in addition, a kind of championship, doubtless in
some measure due to what Keredec had told me
of him, but more to that half-humourous sense of
protectiveness that we always have for those young
people whose untempered and innocent outlook
makes us feel, as we say, "a thousand years old."

The afternoon following our first dinner together,
the two, in returning from their walk, came into
the pavilion with cheerful greetings, instead of
going to their rooms as usual, and Keredec, de-
claring that the open air had "dispersed" his rheumatism, asked if he might overhaul some of my
little canvases and boards. I explained that they
consisted mainly of "notes" for future use, but con-
sented willingly; whereupon he arranged a number
of them as for exhibition and delivered himself
impromptu of the most vehemently instructive lecture on art I had ever heard. Beginning with the
family, the tribe, and the totem-pole, he was able
to demonstrate a theory that art was not only
useful to society but its primary necessity; a curious

thought, probably more attributable to the fact that he was a Frenchman than to that of his being a scientist.

"And here," he said in the course of his demonstration, pointing to a sketch which I had made one morning just after sunrise—"here you can see real sunshine. One certain day there came those few certain moment' at the sunrise when the light was like this. Those few moment', where are they? They have disappeared, gone for eternally. They went"—he snapped his fingers—"like that. Yet here they are—ha!—forever!"

"But it doesn't look like sunshine," said Oliver Saffren hesitatingly, stating a disconcerting but incontrovertible truth; "it only seems to look like it because—isn't it because it's so much brighter than the rest of the picture? I doubt if paint *can* look like sunshine." He turned from the sketch, caught Keredec's gathering frown, and his face flushed painfully. "Ah!" he cried, "I shouldn't have said it?"

I interposed to reassure him, exclaiming that it were a godsend indeed, did all our critics merely speak the plain truth as they see it for themselves. The professor would not have it so, and cut me off.

"No, no, no, my dear sir!" he shouted. "You speak with kindness, but you put some wrong ideas in his head!"

Saffren's look of trouble deepened. "I don't understand," he murmured. " I thought you said always to speak the truth just as I see it."

"I have told you," Keredec declared vehemently, "nothing of the kind!"

"But only yesterday——"

"Never!"

"I understood——"

"Then you understood only one-half! I say, 'Speak the truth as you see it, when you speak.' I did not tell you to speak! How much time have you give' to study sunshine and paint? What do you know about them?"

"Nothing," answered the other humbly.

A profound rumbling was heard, and the frown disappeared from Professor Keredec's brow like the vanishing of the shadow of a little cloud from the dome of some great benevolent and scientific institute. He dropped a weighty hand on his young friend's shoulder, and, in high good-humour, thundered:

"Then you are a critic! Knowing nothing of sunshine except that it warms you, and never having touched paint, you are going to tell about them to a man who spends his life studying them! You look up in the night and the truth you see is that the moon and stars are crossing the ocean. You will tell that to the astronomer? Ha! The truth is what the masters see. When you know what they see, you may speak."

At dinner the night before, it had struck me that Saffren was a rather silent young man by habit, and now I thought I began to understand the reason. I hinted as much, saying, "That would make a quiet world of it."

"All the better, my dear sir!" The professor turned beamingly upon me and continued, dropping into a Whistlerian mannerism that he had sometimes: "You must not blame that great wind of a Keredec for preaching at other people to listen. It gives the poor man more room for himself to talk!"

I found his talk worth hearing.

I would show you, if I could, our pleasant evenings of lingering, after coffee, behind the tremulous screen of honeysuckle, with the night very dark and quiet beyond the warm nimbus of our candle-light, the faces of my two companions clear-obscure in a mellow

shadow like the middle tones of a Rembrandt, and
the professor, good man, talking wonderfully of
everything under the stars and over them,—while
Oliver Saffren and I sat under the spell of the big,
kind voice, the young man listening with the same
eagerness which marked him when he spoke. It
was an eagerness to understand, not to interrupt.

These were our evenings. In the afternoons the
two went for their walk as usual, though now they
did not plunge out of sight of the main road with
the noticeable haste which Amédée had described.
As time pressed, I perceived the caution of Keredec
visibly slackening. Whatever he had feared, the
obscurity and continued quiet of *Les Trois Pigeons*
reassured him; he felt more and more secure in this
sheltered retreat, "far out of the world," and obviously thought no danger imminent. So the days
went by, uneventful for my new friends,—days of
warm idleness for me. Let them go unnarrated; we
pass to the event.

My ankle had taken its wonted time to recover.
I was on my feet again and into the woods—not
traversing, on the way, a certain poppy-sprinkled
field whence a fine Norman stallion snorted ridicule

over a wall. But the fortune of Keredec was to sink as I rose. His summer rheumatism returned, came to grips with him, laid him low. We hobbled together for a day or so, then I threw away my stick and he exchanged his for an improvised crutch. By the time I was fit to run, he was able to do little better than to creep—might well have taken to his bed. But as he insisted that his pupil should not forego the daily long walks and the health of the forest, it came to pass that Saffren often made me the objective of his rambles. At dinner he usually asked in what portion of the forest I should be painting late the next afternoon, and I got in the habit of expecting him to join me toward sunset. We located each other through a code of yodeling that we arranged; his part of these vocal gymnastics being very pleasant to hear, for he had a flexible, rich voice. I shudder to recall how largely my own performances partook of the grotesque. But in the forest where were no musical persons (I supposed) to take hurt from whatever noise I made, I would let go with all the lungs I had; he followed the horrid sounds to their origin, and we would return to the inn together.

On these homeward walks I found him a good

companion, and that is something not to be under-
valued by a selfish man who lives for himself and
his own little ways and his own little thoughts, and
for very little else,—which is the kind of man (as I
have already confessed) that I was—deserving the
pity of all happily or unhappily married persons.

Responsive in kind to either a talkative mood or
a silent one, always gentle in manner, and always
unobtrusively melancholy, Saffren never took the ini-
tiative, though now and then he asked a question
about some rather simple matter which might be
puzzling him.   Whatever the answer, he usually
received it in silence, apparently turning the thing
over and over and inside out in his mind. He was
almost tremulously sensitive, yet not vain, for he
was neither afraid nor ashamed to expose his igno-
rance, his amazing lack of experience.   He had a
greater trouble, one that I had not fathomed. Sometimes there came over his face a look of importunate
wistfulness and distressed perplexity, and he seemed
on the point of breaking out with something that
he wished to tell me—or to ask me, for it might
have been a question—but he always kept it back.
Keredec's training seldom lost its hold upon him.

I had gone back to my glade again, and to the

thin sunshine, which came a little earlier, now that we were deep in July; and one afternoon I sat in the mouth of the path, just where I had played the bounding harlequin for the benefit of the lovely visitor at Quesnay. It was warm in the woods and quiet, warm with the heat of July, still with a July stillness. The leaves had no motion; if there were birds or insects within hearing they must have been asleep; the quivering flight of a butterfly in that languid air seemed, by contrast, quite a commotion; a humming-bird would have made a riot.

I heard the light snapping of a twig and a swish of branches from the direction in which I faced; evidently some one was approaching the glade, though concealed from me for the moment by the winding of the path. Taking it for Saffren, as a matter of course (for we had arranged to meet at that time and place), I raised my voice in what I intended for a merry yodel of greeting.

I yodeled loud, I yodeled long. Knowing my own deficiencies in this art, I had adopted the cunning sinner's policy toward sin and made a joke of it: thus, since my best performance was not unsuggestive of calamity in the poultry yard, I made it worse. And then and there, when my mouth was at its widest in the production of these shocking ulla-hootings, the person approaching came round a turn in the path, and within full sight of me. To my ultimate, utmost horror, it was Madame d'Armand.

I grew so furiously red that it burned me. I had not the courage to run, though I could have prayed that she might take me for what I seemed—plainly a lunatic, whooping the lonely peace of the woods into pandemonium—and turn back. But she kept straight on, must inevitably reach the glade and cross it, and I calculated wretchedly that at the rate she was walking, unhurried but not lagging, it would be about thirty seconds before she passed me. Then suddenly, while I waited in sizzling shame, a clear voice rang out from a distance in an answering yodel to mine, and I thanked heaven for its mercies; at least she would see that my antics had some reason.

She stopped short, in a half-step, as if a little startled, one arm raised to push away a thin green branch that crossed the path at shoulder-height; and her attitude was so charming as she paused, detained to listen by this other voice with its musical youthfulness, that for a second I thought crossly of all the young men in the world.

There was a final call, clear and loud as a bugle,

and she turned to the direction whence it came, so that her back was toward me. Then Oliver Saffren came running lightly round the turn of the path, near her and facing her.

He stopped as short as she had.

Her hand dropped from the slender branch, and pressed against her side.

He lifted his hat and spoke to her, and I thought she made some quick reply in a low voice, though I could not be sure.

She held that startled attitude a moment longer, then turned and crossed the glade so hurriedly that it was almost as if she ran away from him. I had moved aside with my easel and camp-stool, but she passed close to me as she entered the path again on my side of the glade. She did not seem to see me, her dark eyes stared widely straight ahead, her lips were parted, and she looked white and frightened.

She disappeared very quickly in the windings of the path.

CHAPTER IX

HE came on more slowly, his eyes following
her as she vanished, then turning to me
with a rather pitiful apprehension—a
look like that I remember to have seen (some hun-
dreds of years ago) on the face of a freshman,
glancing up from his book to find his doorway
ominously filling with sophomores.

I stepped out to meet him, indignant upon several
counts, most of all upon his own. I knew there was
no offence in his heart, not the remotest rude intent,
but the fact was before me that he had frightened
a woman, had given this very lovely guest of my
friends good cause to hold him a boor, if she did not,
indeed, think him (as she probably thought me) an
outright lunatic! I said:

"You spoke to that lady!" And my voice sounded
unexpectedly harsh and sharp to my own ears, for I
had meant to speak quietly.

"I know—I know. It—it was wrong," he stammered. "I knew I shouldn't—and I couldn't help it."

"You expect me to believe that?"

112

"It's the truth; I couldn't!"

I laughed sceptically; and he flinched, but repeated that what he had said was only the truth. "I don't understand; it was all beyond me," he added huskily.

"What was it you said to her?"

"I spoke her name—'Madame d'Armand.'"

"You said more than that!"

"I asked her if she would let me see her again."

"What else?"

"Nothing," he answered humbly. "And then she —then for a moment it seemed—for a moment she didn't seem to be able to speak——"

"I should think not!" I shouted, and burst out at him with satirical laughter. He stood patiently enduring it, his lowered eyes following the aimless movements of his hands, which were twisting and untwisting his flexible straw hat; and it might have struck me as nearer akin to tragedy rather than to a thing for laughter: this spectacle of a grown man so like a schoolboy before the master, shamefaced over a stammered confession.

"But she did say something to you, didn't she?" I asked finally, with the gentleness of a cross-examining lawyer.

"Yes—after that moment."

"Well, what was it?"

"She said, 'Not now!' That was all."

"I suppose that was all she had breath for! It was just the inconsequent and meaningless thing a frightened woman *would* say!"

"Meaningless?" he repeated, and looked up wonderingly.

"Did you take it for an appointment?" I roared, quite out of patience, and losing my temper completely.

"No, no, no! She said only that, and then——"

"Then she turned and ran away from you!"

"Yes," he said, swallowing painfully.

"That *pleased* you," I stormed, "to frighten a woman in the woods—to make her feel that she can't walk here in safety! You *enjoy* doing things like that?"

He looked at me with disconcerting steadiness for a moment, and, without offering any other response, turned aside, resting his arm against the trunk of a tree and gazing into the quiet forest.

I set about packing my traps, grumbling various sarcasms, the last mutterings of a departed storm, for already I realised that I had taken out my own mortification upon him, and I was stricken with remorse. And yet, so contrarily are we made, I continued to be unkind while in my heart I was asking pardon of him. I tried to make my reproaches gentler, to lend my voice a hint of friendly humour, but in spite of me the one sounded gruffer and the other sourer with everything I said. This was the worse because of the continued silence of the victim: he did not once answer, nor by the slightest movement alter his attitude until I had finished—and more than finished.

"There—and that's all!" I said desperately, when the things were strapped and I had slung them to my shoulder. "Let's be off, in heaven's name!"

At that he turned quickly toward me; it did not lessen my remorse to see that he had grown very pale.

"I wouldn't have frightened her for the world," he said, and his voice and his whole body shook with a strange violence. "I wouldn't have frightened her to please the angels in heaven!"

A blunderer whose incantation had brought the spirit up to face me, I stared at him helplessly, nor could I find words to answer or control the passion that my imbecile scolding had evoked. Whatever the barriers Keredec's training had built for his protection, they were down now.

"You think I told a lie!" he cried. "You think I lied when I said I couldn't help speaking to her!"

"No, no," I said earnestly. "I didn't mean——"

"Words!" he swept the feeble protest away, drowned in a whirling vehemence. "And what does it matter? You *can't* understand. When *you* want to know what to do, you look back into your life and it tells you; and I look back—*ah!*" He cried out, uttering a half-choked, incoherent syllable. "I look back and it's all—BLIND! All these things you *can* do and *can't* do—all these infinite little things! You know, and Keredec knows, and Glouglou knows, and every mortal soul on earth knows—but *I* don't know! Your life has taught you, and you know, but I don't know. I haven't *had* my life. It's gone! All I have is words that Keredec has said to me, and it's like a man with no eyes, out in the sunshine hunting for the light. Do you think words can teach you to resist such impulses as I had when I spoke to Madame d'Armand? Can life itself teach you to resist them? Perhaps you never had them?"

"I don't know," I answered honestly.

"I would burn my hand from my arm and my arm from my body," he went on, with the same wild intensity, "rather than trouble her or frighten her, but I couldn't help speaking to her any more than I can help wanting to see her again—the feeling that I *must*—whatever you say or do, whatever Keredec says or does, whatever the whole world may say or do. And I will! It isn't a thing to choose to do, or not to do. I can't help it any more than I can help being alive!"

He paused, wiping from his brow a heavy dew not of the heat, but like that on the forehead of a man in crucial pain. I made nervous haste to seize the opportunity, and said gently, almost timidly:

"But if it should distress the lady?"

"Yes—then I could keep away. But I must know that."

"I think you might know it by her running away —and by her look," I said mildly. "Didn't you?"

"*No!*" And his eyes flashed an added emphasis.

"Well, well," I said, "let's be on our way, or the professor will be wondering if he is to dine alone."

Without looking to see if he followed, I struck into the path toward home. He did follow, obediently enough, not uttering another word so long as we were in the woods, though I could hear him breathing sharply as he strode behind me, and knew that he was struggling to regain control of himself.

I set the pace, making it as fast as I could, and neither of us spoke again until we had come out of the forest and were upon the main road near the Baudry cottage. Then he said in a steadier voice:

"Why should it distress her?"

"Well, you see," I began, not slackening the pace "there are formalities——"

"Ah, I know," he interrupted, with an impatient laugh. "Keredec once took me to a marionette show —all the little people strung on wires; they couldn't move any other way. And so you mustn't talk to a woman until somebody whose name has been spoken to you speaks yours to her! Do you call that a rule of nature?"

"My dear boy," I laughed in some desperation, "we must conform to it, ordinarily, no matter whose rule it is."

"Do you think Madame d'Armand cares for little forms like that?" he asked challengingly.

"She does," I assured him with perfect confidence. "And, for the hundredth time, you must have seen how you troubled her."

"No," he returned, with the same curious obstinacy, "I don't believe it. There was something, but it wasn't trouble. We looked straight at each other;

I saw her eyes plainly, and it was—" he paused and sighed, a sudden, brilliant smile upon his lips—"it was very—it was very strange!"

There was something so glad and different in his look that—like any other dried-up old blunderer in my place—I felt an instant tendency to laugh. It was that heathenish possession, the old insanity of the risibles, which makes a man think it a humourous thing that his friend should be discovered in love.

But before I spoke, before I quite smiled outright, I was given the grace to see myself in the likeness of a leering stranger trespassing in some cherished inclosure: a garden where the gentlest guests must always be intruders, and only the owner should come. The best of us profane it readily, leaving the coarse prints of our heels upon its paths, mauling and man-handling the fairy blossoms with what pudgy fingers! Comes the poet, ruthlessly leaping the wall and trumpeting indecently his view-halloo of the chase, and, after him, the joker, snickering and hopeful of a kill among the rose-beds; for this has been their hunting-ground since the world began. These two have made us miserably ashamed of the divine infinitive, so that we are afraid to utter the very words "to love," lest some urchin overhear and pursue us with a sticky forefinger and stickier taunts. It is little to my credit that I checked the silly impulse to giggle at the eternal marvel, and went as gently as I could where I should not have gone at all.

"But if you were wrong," I said, "if it did distress her, and if it happened that she has already had too much that was distressing in her life——"

"You know something about her!" he exclaimed. "You know——"

"I do not," I interrupted in turn. "I have only a vague guess; I may be altogether mistaken."

"What is it that you guess?" he demanded abruptly. "Who made her suffer?"

"I think it was her husband," I said, with a lack of discretion for which I was instantly sorry, fearing with reason that I had added a final blunder to the long list of the afternoon. "That is," I added, "if my guess is right."

He stopped short in the road, detaining me by the arm, the question coming like a whip-crack: sharp, loud, violent.

"Is he alive?"

"I don't know," I answered, beginning to move forward; "and this is foolish talk—especially on my part!"

"But I want to know," he persisted, again detaining me.

"And I *don't* know!" I returned emphatically. "Probably I am entirely mistaken in thinking that I know anything of her whatever. I ought not to have spoken, unless I knew what I was talking about, and I'd rather not say any more until I do know."

"Very well," he said quickly. "Will you tell me then?"

"Yes—if you will let it go at that."

"Thank you," he said, and with an impulse which was but too plainly one of gratitude, offered me his hand. I took it, and my soul was disquieted within me, for it was no purpose of mine to set inquiries on foot in regard to the affairs of "Madame d'Armand."

It was early dusk, that hour, a little silvered but still clear, when the edges of things are beginning to grow indefinite, and usually our sleepy countryside knew no tranquiller time of day; but to-night, as we approached the inn, there were strange shapes in the roadway and other tokens that events were stirring there.

From the courtyard came the sounds of laughter and chattering voices. Before the entrance stood a couple of open touring-cars; the chauffeurs engaged in cooling the rear tires with buckets of water brought by a personage ordinarily known as Glouglou, whose look and manner, as he performed this office for the leathern dignitaries, so awed me that I wondered I had ever dared address him with any presumption of intimacy. The cars were great and opulent, of impressive wheel-base, and fore-and-aft they were laden intricately with baggage: concave trunks fitting behind the tonneaus, thin trunks fastened upon the footboards, green, circular trunks adjusted to the spare tires, all deeply coated with dust. Here were fineries from Paris, doubtless on their way to flutter over the gay sands of Trouville, and now wandering but temporarily from the road; for such splendours were never designed to dazzle us of Madame Brossard's.

We were crossing before the machines when one of the drivers saw fit to crank his engine (if that is the knowing phrase) and the thing shook out the usual vibrating uproar. It had a devastating effect upon my companion. He uttered a wild exclamation and sprang sideways into me, almost upsetting us both.

"What on earth is the matter?" I asked. "Did you think the car was starting?"

He turned toward me a face upon which was imprinted the sheer, blank terror of a child. It passed in an instant however, and he laughed.

"I really didn't know. Everything has been so quiet always, out here in the country—and that horrible racket coming so suddenly——"

Laughing with him, I took his arm and we turned to enter the archway. As we did so we almost ran into a tall man who was coming out, evidently intending to speak to one of the drivers.

The stranger stepped back with a word of apology, and I took note of him for a fellow-countryman, and a worldly buck of fashion indeed, almost as cap-a-pie the automobilist as my mysterious spiller of cider had been the pedestrian. But this was no game-chicken; on the contrary (so far as a glance in the dusk of the archway revealed him), much the picture for framing in a club window of a Sunday morning; a seasoned, hard-surfaced, knowing creature for whom many a head waiter must have swept previous claimants from desired tables. He looked forty years so cannily that I guessed him to be about fifty.

We were passing him when he uttered an ejaculation of surprise and stepped forward again, holding out his hand to my companion, and exclaiming:

"Where did *you* come from? I'd hardly have known you."

Oliver seemed unconscious of the proffered hand; he stiffened visibly and said:

"I think there must be some mistake."

"So there is," said the other promptly. "I have been misled by a resemblance. I beg your pardon."

He lifted his cap slightly, going on, and we entered the courtyard to find a cheerful party of nine or ten men and women seated about a couple of tables. Like the person we had just encountered, they all exhibited a picturesque elaboration of the costume permitted by their mode of travel; making effective groupings in their ample draperies of buff and green and white, with glimpses of a flushed and pretty face or two among the loosened veilings. Upon the tables were pots of tea, plates of sandwiches, Madame Brossard's three best silver dishes heaped with fruit, and some bottles of dry champagne from the cellars of Rheims. The partakers were making very merry, having with them (as is inevitable in all such parties, it seems) a fat young man inclined to humour, who was now upon his feet for the proposal of some prankish toast. He interrupted himself long enough to glance our way as we crossed the garden; and it struck me that several pairs of brighter eyes followed my young companion with interest. He was well worth it, perhaps all the more because he was so genuinely unconscious of it; and he ran up the gallery steps and disappeared into his own rooms without sending even a glance from the corner of his eye in return.

I went almost as quickly to my pavilion, and, without lighting my lamp, set about my preparations for dinner.

The party outside, breaking up presently, could be heard moving toward the archway with increased noise and laughter, inspired by some exquisite antic on the part of the fat young man, when a girl's voice (a very attractive voice) called, "Oh, Cressie, aren't you coming?" and a man's replied, from near my veranda: "Only stopping to light a cigar."

A flutter of skirts and a patter of feet betokened that the girl came running back to join the smoker. "Cressie," I heard her say in an eager, lowered tone, "who *was* he?"

"Who was who?"

"That *devastating* creature in white flannels!"

The man chuckled. "Matinée sort of devastator—
what? Monte Cristo hair, noble profile——"

"You'd better tell me," she interrupted earnestly
—"if you don't want me to ask the *waiter*."

"But I don't know him."

"I saw you speak to him."

"I thought it was a man I met three years ago
out in San Francisco, but I was mistaken. There was
a slight resemblance. This fellow might have been
a rather decent younger brother of the man I knew.
He was the——"

My strong impression was that if the speaker
had not been interrupted at this point he would have
said something very unfavourable to the character
of the man he had met in San Francisco; but there
came a series of blasts from the automobile horns
and loud calls from others of the party, who were
evidently waiting for these two.

"Coming!" shouted the man.

"Wait!" said his companion hurriedly. "Who was
the other man, the older one with the painting things
and *such* a coat?"

"Never saw him before in my life."

I caught a last word from the girl as the pair
moved away.

"I'll come back here with a *band* to-morrow night, and serenade the beautiful one.

"Perhaps he'd drop me his card out of the window!"

The horns sounded again; there was a final chorus of laughter, suddenly ceasing to be heard as the cars swept away, and *Les Trois Pigeons* was left to its accustomed quiet.

"Monsieur is served," said Amédée, looking in at my door, five minutes later.

"You have passed a great hour just now, Amédée."

"It was like the old days, truly!"

"They are off for Trouville, I suppose."

"No, monsieur, they are on their way to visit the château, and stopped here only because the run from Paris had made the tires too hot."

"To visit Quesnay, you mean?"

"Truly. But monsieur need give himself no uneasiness; I did not mention to any one that monsieur is here. His name was not spoken. Mademoiselle Ward returned to the château to-day," he added. "She has been in England."

"Quesnay will be gay," I said, coming out to the table. Oliver Saffren was helping the professor down the steps, and Keredec, bent with suffering, but indomitable, gave me a hearty greeting, and began a ruthless dissection of Plato with the soup. Oliver, usually very quiet, as I have said, seemed a little restless under the discourse to-night. However, he did not interrupt, sitting patiently until bedtime, though obviously not listening. When he bade me good night he gave me a look so clearly in reference to a secret understanding between us that, meaning to keep only the letter of my promise to him, I felt about as comfortable as if I had meanly tricked a child.

CHAPTER X

I HAD finished dressing, next morning, and was strapping my things together for the day's campaign, when I heard a shuffling step upon the porch, and the door opened gently, without any previous ceremony of knocking. To my angle of vision what at first appeared to have opened it was a tray of coffee, rolls, eggs, and a packet of sandwiches, but, after hesitating somewhat, this apparition advanced farther into the room, disclosing a pair of supporting hands, followed in due time by the whole person of a nervously smiling and visibly apprehensive Amédée. He closed the door behind him by the simple action of backing against it, took the cloth from his arm, and with a single gesture spread it neatly upon a small table, then, turning to me, laid the forefinger of his right hand warningly upon his lips and bowed me a deferential invitation to occupy the chair beside the table.

"Well," I said, glaring at him, "what ails you?"

"I thought monsieur might prefer his breakfast indoors, this morning," he returned in a low voice

"Why should I?"

The miserable old man said something I did not understand—an incoherent syllable or two—suddenly covered his mouth with both hands, and turned away. I heard a catch in his throat; suffocated sounds issued from his bosom; however, it was nothing more than a momentary seizure, and, recovering command of himself by a powerful effort, he faced me with hypocritical servility.

"Why do you laugh?" I asked indignantly.

"But I did not laugh," he replied in a husky whisper. "Not at all."

"You did," I asserted, raising my voice. "It almost killed you!"

"Monsieur," he begged hoarsely, "*hush!*"

"What is the matter?" I demanded loudly. "What do you mean by these abominable croakings? Speak out!"

"Monsieur—" he gesticulated in a panic, toward the courtyard. "Mademoiselle Ward is out there."

"*What!*" But I did not shout the word.

"There is always a little window in the rear wall" he breathed in my ear as I dropped into the chair by the table. "She would not see you if——"

I interrupted with all the French rough-and-ready expressions of dislike at my command, daring to hope that they might give him some shadowy, far-away idea of what I thought of both himself and his suggestions, and, notwithstanding the difficulty of expressing strong feeling in whispers, it seemed to me that, in a measure, I succeeded. "I am not in the habit of crawling out of ventilators," I added, subduing a tendency to vehemence. "And probably Mademoiselle Ward has only come to talk with Madame Brossard."

"I fear some of those people may have told her you were here," he ventured insinuatingly.

"What people?" I asked, drinking my coffee calmly, yet, it must be confessed, without quite the deliberation I could have wished.

"Those who stopped yesterday evening on the way to the château. They might have recognised——"

"Impossible. I knew none of them."

"But Mademoiselle Ward knows that you are here. Without doubt."

"Why do you say so?"

"Because she has inquired for you."

"So!" I rose at once and went toward the door. "Why didn't you tell me at once?"

"But surely," he remonstrated, ignoring my

question, "monsieur will make some change of attire?"

"Change of attire?" I echoed.

"Eh, the poor old coat all hunched at the shoulders and spotted with paint!"

"Why shouldn't it be?" I hissed, thoroughly irritated. "Do you take me for a racing marquis?"

"But monsieur has a coat much more as a coat ought to be. And Jean Ferret says——"

"Ha, now we're getting at it!" said I. "What does Jean Ferret say?"

"Perhaps it would be better if I did not repeat——"

"Out with it! What does Jean Ferret say?"

"Well, then, Mademoiselle Ward's maid from Paris has told Jean Ferret that monsieur and Mademoiselle Ward have corresponded for years, and that—and that——"

"Go on," I bade him ominously.

"That monsieur has sent Mademoiselle Ward many expensive jewels, and——"

"Aha!" said I, at which he paused abruptly, and stood staring at me. The idea of explaining Miss Elizabeth's collection to him, of getting any-

thing whatever through that complacent head of
his, was so hopeless that I did not even consider
it. There was only one thing to do, and perhaps I
should have done it—I do not know, for he saw
the menace coiling in my eye, and hurriedly re-
treated.

"Monsieur!" he gasped, backing away from me,
and as his hand, fumbling behind him, found
the latch of the door, he opened it, and scrambled
out by a sort of spiral movement round the casing.
When I followed, a moment later—with my traps
on my shoulder and the packet of sandwiches in
my pocket—he was out of sight.

Miss Elizabeth sat beneath the arbour at the
other end of the courtyard, and beside her stood
the trim and glossy bay saddle-horse that she had
ridden from Quesnay, his head outstretched above
his mistress to paddle at the vine leaves with a tremulous upper lip. She checked his desire with a
slight movement of her hand upon the bridle-rein;
and he arched his neck prettily, pawing the gravel
with a neat forefoot. Miss Elizabeth is one of the
few large women I have known to whom a riding-
habit is entirely becoming, and this group of two—
a handsome woman and her handsome horse—has

had a charm for all men ever since horses were tamed and women began to be beautiful. I thought of my work, of the canvases I meant to cover, but I felt the charm—and I felt it stirringly. It was a fine, fresh morning, and the sun just risen.

An expression in the lady's attitude, and air which I instinctively construed as histrionic, seemed intended to convey that she had been kept waiting, yet had waited without reproach; and although she must have heard me coming, she did not look toward me until I was quite near and spoke her name. At that she sprang up quickly enough, and stretched out her hand to me.

"Run to earth!" she cried, advancing a step to meet me.

"A pretty poor trophy of the chase," said I, "but proud that you are its killer."

To my surprise and mystification, her cheeks and brow flushed rosily; she was obviously conscious of it, and laughed.

"Don't be embarrassed," she said.

"I!"

"Yes, you, poor man! I suppose I couldn't have more thoroughly compromised you. Madame Brossard will never believe in your respectability again."

"Oh, yes, she will," said I.

"What? A lodger who has ladies calling upon him at five o'clock in the morning? But your bundle's on your shoulder," she rattled on, laughing, "though there's many could be bolder, and perhaps you'll let me walk a bit of the way with you, if you're for the road."

"Perhaps I will," said I. She caught up her riding-skirt, fastening it by a clasp at her side, and we passed out through the archway and went slowly along the road bordering the forest, her horse following obediently at half-rein's length.

"When did you hear that I was at Madame Brossard's?" I asked.

"Ten minutes after I returned to Quesnay, late yesterday afternoon."

"Who told you?"

"Louise."

I repeated the name questioningly. "You mean Mrs. Larrabee Harman?"

"Louise Harman," she corrected. "Didn't you know she was staying at Quesnay?"

"I guessed it, though Amédée got the name confused."

"Yes, she's been kind enough to look after the

place for us while we were away. George won't
be back for another ten days, and I've been over-
seeing an exhibition for him in London. Afterward I did a round of visits—tiresome enough, but
among people it's well to keep in touch with on
George's account."

"I see," I said, with a grimness which probably
escaped her. "But how did Mrs. Harman know
that I was at *Les Trois Pigeons*?"

"She met you once in the forest——"

"Twice," I interrupted.

"She mentioned only once. Of course she'd often
heard both George and me speak of you."

"But how did she know it was I and where I
was staying?"

"Oh, that?" Her smile changed to a laugh.
"Your *maître d'hôtel* told Ferret, a gardener at
Quesnay, that you were at the inn."

"He did!"

"Oh, but you mustn't be angry with him; he made
it quite all right."

"How did he do that?" I asked, trying to speak
calmly, though there was that in my mind which
might have blanched the parchment cheek of a
grand inquisitor.

"He told Ferret that you were very anxious not to have it known——"

"You call that making it all right?"

"For himself, I mean. He asked Ferret not to mention who it was that told him."

"The rascal!" I cried. "The treacherous, brazen——"

"Unfortunate man," said Miss Elizabeth, "don't you see how clear you're making it that you really meant to hide from us?"

There seemed to be something in that, and my tirade broke up in confusion. "Oh, no," I said lamely, "I hoped—I hoped——"

"Be careful!"

"No; I hoped to work down here," I blurted. "And I thought if I saw too much of you—I might not."

She looked at me with widening eyes. "And I can take my choice," she cried, "of all the different things you may mean by that! It's either the most outrageous speech I ever heard—or the most flattering."

"But I meant simply——"

"No." She lifted her hand and stopped me. "I'd rather believe that I have at least the choice

—and let it go at that." And as I began to laugh, she turned to me with a gravity apparently so genuine that for the moment I was fatuous enough to believe that she had said it seriously. Ensued a pause of some duration, which, for my part, I found disturbing. She broke it with a change of subject.

"You think Louise very lovely to look at, don't you?"

"Exquisite," I answered.

"Every one does."

"I suppose she told you—" and now I felt myself growing red—"that I behaved like a drunken acrobat when she came upon me in the path."

"No. Did you?" cried Miss Elizabeth, with a ready credulity which I thought by no means pretty; indeed, she seemed amused and, to my surprise (for she is not an unkind woman), rather heartlessly pleased. "Louise only said she knew it must be you, and that she wished she could have had a better look at what you were painting."

"Heaven bless her!" I exclaimed. "Her reticence was angelic."

"Yes, she has reticence," said my companion, with enough of the same quality to make me look at her quickly. A thin line had been drawn across her forehead.

"You mean she's still reticent with George?" I ventured.

"Yes," she answered sadly. "Poor George always hopes, of course, in the silent way of his kind when they suffer from such unfortunate passions—and he waits."

"I suppose that former husband of hers recovered?"

"I believe he's still alive somewhere. Locked up, I hope!" she finished crisply.

"She retained his name," I observed.

"Harman? Yes, she retained it," said my companion rather shortly.

"At all events, she's rid of him, isn't she?"

"Oh, she's *rid* of him!" Her tone implied an enigmatic reservation of some kind.

"It's hard," I reflected aloud. "hard to understand her making that mistake, young as she was. Even in the glimpses of her I've had, it was easy to see something of what she's like: a fine, rare, high type——"

"But you didn't know *him*, did you?" Miss Elizabeth asked with some dryness.

"No," I answered. "I saw him twice; once at the time of his accident—that was only a nightmare, his face covered with—" I shivered. "But I had caught a glimpse of him on the boulevard, and of all the dreadful——"

"Oh, but he wasn't always dreadful," she interposed quickly. "He was a fascinating sort of person, quite charming and good-looking, when she ran away with him, though he was horribly dissipated even then. He always had been *that*. Of course she thought she'd be able to straighten him out —poor girl! She tried, for three years—three years it hurts one to think of! You see it must have been something very like a 'grand passion' to hold her through a pain three years long."

"Or tremendous pride," said I. "Women make an odd world of it for the rest of us. There was good old George, as true and straight a man as ever lived——"

"And she took the other! Yes." George's sister laughed sorrowfully.

"But George and she have both survived the mistake," I went on with confidence. "Her tragedy must have taught her some important differences. Haven't you a notion she'll be tremendously glad to see him when he comes back from America?"

"Ah, I do hope so!" she cried. "You see, I'm fearing that he hopes so too—to the degree of counting on it."

"You don't count on it yourself?"

She shook her head. "With any other woman I should."

"Why not with Mrs. Harman?"

"Cousin Louise has her ways," said Miss Elizabeth slowly, and, whether she could not further explain her doubts, or whether she would not, that was all I got out of her on the subject at the time. I asked one or two more questions, but my companion merely shook her head again, alluding vaguely to her cousin's "ways." Then she brightened suddenly, and inquired when I would have my things sent up to the château from the inn.

At the risk of a misunderstanding which I felt I could ill afford, I resisted her kind hospitality, and the outcome of it was that there should be a kind of armistice, to begin with my dining at the château that evening. Thereupon she mounted to the saddle, a bit of gymnastics for which she de-

clined my assistance, and looked down upon me
from a great height.

"Did anybody ever tell you," was her surprising
inquiry, "that you are the queerest man of these
times?"

"No," I answered. "Don't you think you're a
queerer woman?"

"*Footle!*" she cried scornfully. "Be off to your
woods and your woodscaping!"

The bay horse departed at a smart gait, not, I
was glad to see, a parkish trot—Miss Elizabeth
wisely set limits to her sacrifices to Mode—and she
was far down the road before I had passed the outer
fringe of trees.

My work was accomplished after a fashion more
or less desultory that day; I had many absent
moments, was restless, and walked more than I
painted. Oliver Saffren did not join me in the
late afternoon; nor did the echo of distant yodelling
bespeak any effort on his part to find me. So I
gave him up, and returned to the inn earlier than
usual.

While dressing I sent word to Professor Keredec
that I should not be able to join him at dinner
that evening; and it is to be recorded that Glouglou

carried the message for me.   Amédée did not appear, from which it may be inferred that our *maître d'hôtel* was subject to lucid intervals.   Certainly his present shyness indicated an intelligence of no low order.

CHAPTER XI

THE dining-room at Quesnay is a pretty work of the second of those three Louises who made so much furniture. It was never a proper setting for a rusty, out-of-doors painter-man, nor has such a fellow ever found himself complacently at ease there since the day its first banquet was spread for a score or so of fine-feathered epigram jinglers, fiddling Versailles gossip out of a rouge-and-lace Quesnay marquise newly sent into half-earnest banishment for too much king-hunting. For my part, however, I should have preferred a chance at making a place for myself among the wigs and brocades to the Crusoe's Isle of my chair at Miss Elizabeth's table.

I learned at an early age to look my vanities in the face; I outfaced them and they quailed, but persisted, surviving for my discomfort to this day. Here is the confession: It was not until my arrival at the château that I realised what temerity it involved to dine there in evening clothes purchased, some four or five or six years previously, in the economical neighbourhood of the Boulevard St. Michel. Yet the things fitted me well enough; were clean and not shiny, having been worn no more than a dozen times, I think; though they might have been better pressed.

Looking over the men of the Quesnay party—or perhaps I should signify a reversal of that and say a glance of theirs at me—revealed the importance of a particular length of coat-tail, of a certain rich effect obtained by widely separating the lower points of the waistcoat, of the display of some imagination in the buttons upon the same garment, of a doubled-back arrangement of cuffs, and of a specific design and dimension of tie. Marked uniformity in these matters denoted their necessity; and clothes differing from the essential so vitally as did mine must have seemed immodest, little better than no clothes at all. I doubt if I could have argued in extenuation my lack of advantages for study, such an excuse being itself the damning circumstance. Of course eccentricity is permitted, but (as in the Arts) only to the established. And I recall a painful change of colour which befell the countenance of a shining young man I met at Ward's house in Paris: he had used his handkerchief and was ab-

sently putting it in his pocket when he providen‹
tially noticed what he was doing and restored it
to his sleeve.

Miss Elizabeth had the courage to take me under
her wing, placing me upon her left at dinner; but
sprightlier calls than mine demanded and occupied
her attention. At my other side sat a magnificently
upholstered lady, who offered a fine shoulder and
the rear wall of a collar of pearls for my observation throughout the evening, as she leaned forward
talking eagerly with a male personage across the
table. This was a prince, ending in "ski": he
permitted himself the slight vagary of wearing a
gold bracelet, and perhaps this flavour of romance
drew the lady. Had my good fortune ever granted
a second meeting, I should not have known her.

Fragments reaching me in my seclusion indicated
that the various conversations up and down the
long table were animated; and at times some topic
proved of such high interest as to engage the comment of the whole company. This was the case
when the age of one of the English king's grand-
children came in question, but a subject which
called for even longer (if less spirited) discourse
concerned the shameful lack of standard on the

part of citizens of the United States, or, as it was put, with no little exasperation, "What *is* the trouble with America?" Hereupon brightly gleamed the fat young man whom I had marked for a wit at *Les Trois Pigeons;* he pictured with inimitable mimicry a western senator lately in France. This outcast, it appeared, had worn a slouch hat at a garden party and had otherwise betrayed his country to the ridicule of the intelligent. "But really," said the fat young man, turning plaintiff in conclusion, "imagine what such things make the English and the French think of *us!*" And it finally went by consent that the trouble with America was the vulgarity of our tourists.

"A dreadful lot!" Miss Elizabeth cheerfully summed up for them all. "The miseries I undergo with that class of 'prominent Amurricans' who bring letters to my brother! I remember one awful creature who said, when I came into the room, 'Well, ma'am, I guess you're the lady of the house, aren't you?'"

Miss Elizabeth sparkled through the chorus of laughter, but I remembered the "awful creature," a genial and wise old man of affairs, whose daughter's portrait George painted. Miss Elizabeth had missed his point: the canvasser's phrase had been intended with humour, and even had it lacked that, it was not without a pretty quaintness. So I thought, being "left to my own reflections," which may have partaken of my own special kind of snobbery; at least I regretted the Elizabeth of the morning garden and the early walk along the fringe of the woods. For she at my side to-night was another lady.

The banquet was drawing to a close when she leaned toward me and spoke in an undertone. As this was the first sign, in so protracted a period, that I might ever again establish relations with the world of men, it came upon me like a Friday's footprint, and in the moment of shock I did not catch what she said.

"Anne Elliott, yonder, is asking you a question," she repeated, nodding at a very pretty girl down and across the table from me. Miss Anne Elliott's attractive voice had previously enabled me to recognise her as the young woman who had threatened to serenade *Les Trois Pigeons*.

"I beg your pardon," I said, addressing her, and at the sound my obscurity was illuminated, about half of the company turning to look at me with wide-eyed surprise. (I spoke in an ordinary tone, it may need to be explained, and there is nothing remarkable about my voice).

"I hear you're at *Les Trois Pigeons*," said Miss Elliott.

"Yes?"

"*Would* you mind telling us something of the *mysterious* Narcissus?"

"If you'll be more definite," I returned, in the tone of a question.

"There couldn't be more than one like *that*," said Miss Elliott, "at least, not in one neighbourhood, could there? I mean a *recklessly* charming vision with a *white* tie and *white* hair and *white* flannels."

"Oh," said I, "*he's* not mysterious."

"But he *is*," she returned; "I insist on his being *mysterious*! Rarely, grandly, *strangely* mysterious! You *will* let me think so?" This young lady had a whimsical manner of emphasising words unexpectedly, with a breathless intensity that approached violence, a habit dangerously contagious among nervous persons, so that I answered slowly, out of a fear that I might echo it.

"It would need a great deal of imagination.

He's a young American, very attractive, very simple——"

"But he's *mad!*" she interrupted.

"Oh, no!" I said hastily.

"But he *is!* A person told me so in a garden this *very* afternoon," she went on eagerly; "a person with a rake and *ever* so many moles on his chin. This person told me all about him. His name is Oliver Saffren, and he's in the charge of a *very* large doctor and quite, *quite* mad!"

"Jean Ferret, the gardener," I said deliberately, and with venom, "is fast acquiring notoriety in these parts as an idiot of purest ray, and he had his information from another whose continuance unhanged is every hour more miraculous."

"How *ruthless* of you," cried Miss Elliott, with exaggerated reproach, "when I have had such a thrilling happiness all day in believing that *riotously* beautiful creature mad! You are wholly positive he isn't?"

Our dialogue was now all that delayed a general departure from the table. This, combined with the naïve surprise I have mentioned, served to make us temporarily the centre of attention, and, among the faces turned toward me, my glance fell unexpectedly upon one I had not seen since entering the dining-room. Mrs. Harman had been placed at some distance from me and on the same side of the table, but now she leaned far back in her chair to look at me, so that I saw her behind the shoulders of the people between us. She was watching me with an expression unmistakably of repressed anxiety and excitement, and as our eyes met, hers shone with a certain agitation, as of some odd consciousness shared with me. It was so strangely, suddenly a reminder of the look of secret understanding given me with good night, twenty-four hours earlier, by the man whose sanity was Miss Elliott's topic, that, puzzled and almost disconcerted for the moment, I did not at once reply to the lively young lady's question.

"You're hesitating!" she cried, clasping her hands. "I believe there's a *darling* little chance of it, after all! And if it weren't so, why would he need to be watched over, day *and* night, by an *enormous* doctor?"

"This *is* romance!" I retorted. "The doctor is Professor Keredec, illustriously known in this country, but not as a physician, and they are following some form of scientific research together, I believe. But, assuming to speak as Mr. Saffren's friend," I added, rising with the others upon Miss Ward's example, "I'm sure if he could come to know of your interest, he would much rather play Hamlet for you than let you find him disappointing."

"If he could come to know of my interest!" she echoed, glancing down at herself with mock demureness. "Don't you think he could come to know something more of me than that?"

The windows had been thrown open, allowing passage to a veranda. Miss Elizabeth led the way outdoors with the prince, the rest of us following at hazard, and in the mild confusion of this withdrawal I caught a final glimpse of Mrs. Harman, which revealed that she was still looking at me with the same tensity; but with the movement of intervening groups I lost her. Miss Elliott pointedly waited for me until I came round the table, attached me definitely by taking my arm, accompanying her action with a dazzling smile. "Oh, *do* you think you can manage it?" she whispered rapturously, to which I replied—as vaguely as I could—that the demands of scientific research upon the time of its followers were apt to be exorbitant.

Tables and coffee were waiting on the broad terrace below, with a big moon rising in the sky. I descended the steps in charge of this pretty cavalier, allowed her to seat me at the most remote of the tables, and accepted without unwillingness other gallantries of hers in the matter of coffee and cigarettes. "And now," she said, "now that I've done so much for your *dearest* hopes and comfort, look up at the milky moon, and tell me *all!*"

"If you can bear it?"

She leaned an elbow on the marble railing that protected the terrace, and, shielding her eyes from the moonlight with her hand, affected to gaze at me dramatically. "Have no distrust," she bade me. "Who and *what* is the glorious stranger?"

Resisting an impulse to chime in with her humour, I gave her so dry and commonplace an account of my young friend at the inn that I presently found myself abandoned to solitude again.

"I don't know where to go," she complained as she rose. "These other people are *most* painful to a girl of my intelligence, but I cannot linger by your side; untruth long ago lost its interest for me, and I prefer to believe Mr. Jean Ferret—if that is the gentleman's name. I'd join Miss Ward and Cressie Ingle yonder, but Cressie *would* be indignant! I shall soothe my hurt with *sweetest* airs. Adieu."

With that she made me a solemn courtesy and
departed, a pretty little figure, not little in attractiveness, the strong moonlight, tinged with blue,
shimmering over her blond hair and splashing
brightly among the ripples of her silks and laces.
She swept across the terrace languidly, offering an
effect of comedy not unfairylike, and, ascending
the steps of the veranda, disappeared into the
orange candle-light of a salon. A moment later
some chords were sounded firmly upon a piano in
that room, and a bitter song swam out to me over
the laughter and talk of the people at the other
tables. It was to be observed that Miss Anne
Elliott sang very well, though I thought she over-
emphasised one line of the stanza:

"This world is a world of lies!"

Perhaps she had poisoned another little arrow
for me, too. Impelled by the fine night, the groups
upon the terrace were tending toward a wider
dispersal, drifting over the sloping lawns by threes
and couples, and I was able to identify two figures
threading the paths of the garden, together, some
distance below. Judging by the pace they kept,
I should have concluded that Miss Ward and
Mr. Cresson Ingle sought the healthful effects of

exercise. However, I could see no good reason
for wishing their conversation less obviously absorbing, though Miss Elliott's insinuation that Mr.
Ingle might deplore intrusion upon the interview
had struck me as too definite to be altogether
pleasing. Still, such matters could not discontent
me with my solitude. Eastward, over the moon-
lit roof of the forest, I could see the quiet ocean,
its unending lines of foam moving slowly to the
long beaches, too far away to be heard. The re-
proachful voice of the singer came no more from
the house, but the piano ran on into "La Vie
de Bohème," and out of that into something else,
I did not know what, but it seemed to be music;
at least it was musical enough to bring before me
some memory of the faces of pretty girls I had
danced with long ago in my dancing days, so that,
what with the music, and the distant sea, and the
soft air, so sparklingly full of moonshine, and the
little dancing memories, I was floated off into a
reverie that was like a prelude for the person who
broke it. She came so quietly that I did not hear
her until she was almost beside me and spoke to me.
It was the second time that had happened.

CHAPTER XII

"MRS. HARMAN," I said, as she took the chair vacated by the elfin young lady, "you see I *can* manage it! But perhaps I control myself better when there's no camp-stool to inspire me. You remember my woodland didoes —I fear?"

She smiled in a pleasant, comprehending way, but neither directly replied nor made any return speech whatever; instead, she let her forearms rest on the broad railing of the marble balustrade, and, leaning forward, gazed out over the shining and mysterious slopes below. Somehow it seemed to me that her not answering, and her quiet action, as well as the thoughtful attitude in which it culminated, would have been thought "very like her" by any one who knew her well. "Cousin Louise has her ways," Miss Elizabeth had told me; this was probably one of them, and I found it singularly attractive. For that matter, from the day of my first sight of her in the woods I had needed no prophet to tell me I should like Mrs. Harman's ways.

156

"After the quiet you have had here, all this must seem," I said, looking down upon the strollers, "a usurpation."

"Oh, *they!*" She disposed of Quesnay's guests with a slight movement of her left hand. "You're an old friend of my cousins—of both of them; but even without that, I know you understand. Elizabeth does it all for her brother, of course."

"But she likes it," I said.

"And Mr. Ward likes it, too," she added slowly. "You'll see, when he comes home."

Night's effect upon me being always to make me venturesome, I took a chance, and ventured perhaps too far. "I hope we'll see many happy things when he comes home."

"It's her doing things of this sort," she said, giving no sign of having heard my remark, "that has helped so much to make him the success that he is."

"It's what has been death to his art!" I exclaimed, too quickly—and would have been glad to recall the speech.

She met it with a murmur of low laughter that sounded pitying. "Wasn't it always a dubious relation—between him and art?" And without await-

ing an answer, she went on, "So it's all the better
that he can have his success!"

To this I had nothing whatever to say. So far
as I remembered, I had never before heard a woman
put so much comprehension of a large subject into
so few words, but in my capacity as George's friend,
hopeful for his happiness, it made me a little uneasy.
During the ensuing pause this feeling, at first
uppermost, gave way to another not at all in se-
quence, but irresponsible and intuitive, that she
had something in particular to say to me, had joined
me for that purpose, and was awaiting the opportunity. As I have made open confession, my
curiosity never needed the spur; and there is no
denying that this impression set it off on the gallop;
but evidently the moment had not come for her
to speak. She seemed content to gaze out over
the valley in silence.

"Mr. Cresson Ingle," I hazarded; "is he an old,
new friend of your cousins? I think he was not
above the horizon when I went to Capri, two
years ago?"

"He wants Elizabeth," she returned, adding
quietly, "as you've seen." And when I had verified
this assumption with a monosyllable, she continued,

CHAPTER TWELVE   159

"He's an 'available,' but I should hate to have it happen. He's hard."

"He doesn't seem very hard toward her," I murmured, looking down into the garden where Mr. Ingle just then happened to be adjusting a scarf about his hostess's shoulders.

"He's led a detestable life," said Mrs. Harman, "among detestable people!"

She spoke with sudden, remarkable vigour, and as if she knew. The full-throated emphasis she put upon "detestable" gave the word the sting of a flagellation; it rang with a rightful indignation that brought vividly to my mind the thought of those three years in Mrs. Harman's life which Elizabeth said "hurt one to think of." For this was the lady who had rejected good George Ward to run away with a man much deeper in all that was detestable than Mr. Cresson Ingle could ever be!

"He seems to me much of a type with these others," I said.

"Oh, they keep their surfaces about the same."

"It made me wish *I* had a little more surface to-night," I laughed. "I'd have fitted better. Miss Ward is different at different times. When we are alone together she always hás the air of excusing, or at least explaining, these people to me, but this evening I've had the disquieting thought that perhaps she also explained me to them."

"Oh, no!" said Mrs. Harman, turning to me quickly. "Didn't you see? She was making up to Mr. Ingle for this morning. It came out that she'd ridden over at daylight to see you; Anne Elliott discovered it in some way and told him."

This presented an aspect of things so overwhelmingly novel that out of a confusion of ideas I was able to fasten on only one with which to continue the conversation, and I said irrelevantly that Miss Elliott was a remarkable young woman. At this my companion, who had renewed her observation of the valley, gave me a full, clear look of earnest scrutiny, which set me on the alert, for I thought that now what she desired to say was coming. But I was disappointed, for she spoke lightly, with a ripple of amusement.

"I suppose she finished her investigations? You told her all you could?"

"Almost."

"I suppose you wouldn't trust *me* with the reservation?" she asked, smiling.

"I would trust you with anything," I answered seriously.

"You didn't gratify that child?" she said, half laughing. Then, to my surprise, her tone changed suddenly, and she began again in a hurried low voice: "You didn't tell her—" and stopped there, breathless and troubled, letting me see that I had been right after all: this was what she wanted to talk about.

"I didn't tell her that young Saffren is mad, no; if that is what you mean."

"I'm glad you didn't," she said slowly, sinking back in her chair so that her face was in the shadow of the awning which sheltered the little table between us.

"In the first place, I wouldn't have told her even if it were true," I returned, "and in the second, it isn't true—though *you* have some reason to think it is," I added.

"*I?*" she said. "Why?"

"His speaking to you as he did; a thing on the face of it inexcusable——"

"Why did he call me 'Madame d'Armand'?" she interposed.

I explained something of the mental processes of Amédée, and she listened till I had finished; then bade me continue.

"That's all," I said blankly, but, with a second thought, caught her meaning. "Oh, about young Saffren, you mean?"

"Yes."

"I know him pretty well," I said, "without really knowing anything about him; but what is stranger, I believe he doesn't really know a great deal about himself. Of course I have a theory about him, though it's vague. My idea is that probably through some great illness he lost—not his faculty of memory, but his memories, or, at least, most of them. In regard to what he does remember, Professor Keredec has anxiously impressed upon him some very poignant necessity for reticence. What the necessity may be, or the nature of the professor's anxieties, I do not know, but I think Keredec's reasons must be good ones. That's all, except that there's something about the young man that draws one to him: I couldn't tell you how much I like him, nor how sorry I am that he offended you."

"He didn't offend me," she murmured—almost whispered.

"He didn't mean to," I said warmly. "You understood that?"

"Yes, I understood."

"I am glad. I'd been waiting the chance to try to explain—to ask you to pardon him——"

"But there wasn't any need."

"You mean because you understood——"

"No," she interrupted gently, "not only that. I mean because he has done it himself."

"Asked your pardon?" I said, in complete surprise.

"Yes."

"He's written you?" I cried.

"No. I saw him to-day," she answered. "This afternoon when I went for my walk, he was waiting where the the paths intersect——"

Some hasty ejaculation, I do not know what, came from me, but she lifted her hand.

"Wait," she said quietly. "As soon as he saw me he came straight toward me——"

"Oh, but this won't do at all," I broke out. "It's too bad——"

"Wait." She leaned forward slightly, lifting her hand again. "He called me 'Madame d'Armand,' and said he must know if he had offended me."

"You told him——"

"I told him 'No!' " And it seemed to me that

her voice, which up to this point had been low but
very steady, shook upon the monosyllable. "He
walked with me a little way—perhaps it was
longer——"

"Trust me that it sha'n't happen again!" I
exclaimed. "I'll see that Keredec knows of this at
once. He will——"

"No, no," she interrupted quickly, "that is
just what I want you not to do. Will you promise
me?"

"I'll promise anything you ask me. But didn't
he frighten you? Didn't he talk wildly? Didn't
he——"

"He didn't frighten me—not as you mean. He
was very quiet and—" She broke off unexpectedly,
with a little pitying cry, and turned to me, lifting
both hands appealingly—"And oh, doesn't he make
one *sorry* for him!"

That was just it. She had gone straight to the
heart of his mystery: his strangeness was the strange
pathos that invested him; the "singularity" of
"that other monsieur" was solved for me at
last.

When she had spoken she rose, advanced a step,
and stood looking out over the valley again, her

skirts pressing the balustrade. One of the moments in my life when I have wished to be a figure painter came then, as she raised her arms, the sleeves, of some filmy texture, falling back from them with the gesture, and clasped her hands lightly behind her neck, the graceful angle of her chin uplifted to the full rain of moonshine. Little Miss Elliott, in the glamour of these same blue showerings, had borrowed gauzy weavings of the fay and the sprite, but Mrs. Harman—tall, straight, delicate to fragility, yet not to thinness—was transfigured with a deeper meaning, wearing the sadder, richer colours of the tragedy that her cruel young romance had put upon her. She might have posed as she stood against the marble railing—and especially in that gesture of lifting her arms—for a bearer of the gift at some foredestined luckless ceremony of votive offerings. So it seemed, at least, to the eyes of a moon-dazed old painter-man.

She stood in profile to me; there were some jasmine flowers at her breast; I could see them rise and fall with more than deep breathing; and I wondered what the man who had talked of her so wildly, only yesterday, would feel if he could know that already the thought of him had moved her.

"I haven't *had* my life. It's gone!" It was almost as if I heard his voice, close at hand, with all the passion of regret and protest that rang in the words when they broke from him in the forest. And by some miraculous conjecture, within the moment I seemed not only to hear his voice but actually to see him, a figure dressed in white, far below us and small with the distance, standing out in the moonlight in the middle of the tree-bordered avenue leading to the château gates.

I rose and leaned over the railing. There was no doubt about the reality of the figure in white, though it was too far away to be identified with certainty; and as I rubbed my eyes for clearer sight, it turned and disappeared into the shadows of the orderly grove where I had stood, one day, to watch Louise Harman ascend the slopes of Quesnay.

But I told myself, sensibly, that more than one man on the coast of Normandy might be wearing white flannels that evening, and, turning to my companion, found that she had moved some steps away from me and was gazing eastward to the sea. I concluded that she had not seen the figure.

"I have a request to make of you," she said, as

"I haven't had my life. It's gone"

I turned. "Will you do it for me—setting it down just as a whim, if you like, and letting it go at that?"

"Yes, I will," I answered promptly. "I'll do anything you ask."

She stepped closer, looked at me intently for a second, bit her lip in indecision, then said, all in a breath:

"Don't tell Mr. Saffren my name!"

"But I hadn't meant to," I protested.

"Don't speak of me to him at all," she said, with the same hurried eagerness. "Will you let me have my way?"

"Could there be any question of that?" I replied, and to my astonishment found that we had somehow impulsively taken each other's hands, as upon a serious bargain struck between us.

CHAPTER XIII

THE round moon was white and at its smallest, high overhead, when I stepped out of the phaeton in which Miss Elizabeth sent me back to Madame Brossard's; midnight was twanging from a rusty old clock indoors as I crossed the fragrant courtyard to my pavilion; but a lamp still burned in the salon of the "Grande Suite," a light to my mind more suggestive of the patient watcher than of the scholar at his tome.

When my own lamp was extinguished, I set my door ajar, moved my bed out from the wall to catch whatever breeze might stir, "composed myself for the night," as it used to be written, and lay looking out upon the quiet garden where a thin white haze was rising. If, in taking this coign of vantage, I had any subtler purpose than to seek a draught against the warmth of the night, it did not fail of its reward, for just as I had begun to drowse, the gallery steps creaked as if beneath some immoderate weight, and the noble form of Keredec emerged upon my field of vision. From the absence of the sound of footsteps I supposed him to be either barefooted or in his stockings. His visible costume consisted of a sleeping jacket tucked into a pair of trousers, while his tousled hair and beard and generally tossed and rumpled look were those of a man who had been lying down temporarily.

I heard him sigh—like one sighing for sleep—as he went noiselessly across the garden and out through the archway to the road. At that I sat straight up in bed to stare—and well I might, for here was a miracle! He had lifted his arms above his head to stretch himself comfortably, and he walked upright and at ease, whereas when I had last seen him, the night before, he had been able to do little more than crawl, bent far over and leaning painfully upon his friend. Never man beheld a more astonishing recovery from a bad case of rheumatism!

After a long look down the road, he retraced his steps; and the moonlight, striking across his great forehead as he came, revealed the furrows ploughed there by an anxiety of which I guessed the cause. The creaking of the wooden stairs and gallery and the whine of an old door announced that he had returned to his vigil.

I had, perhaps, a quarter of an hour to consider this performance, when it was repeated; now, however, he only glanced out into the road, retreating hastily, and I saw that he was smiling, while the speed he maintained in returning to his quarters was remarkable for one so newly convalescent.

The next moment Saffren came through the archway, ascended the steps in turn—but slowly and carefully, as if fearful of waking his guardian—and I heard his door closing, very gently. Long before his arrival, however, I had been certain of his identity with the figure I had seen gazing up at the terraces of Quesnay from the borders of the grove. Other questions remained to bother me: Why had Keredec not prevented this night-roving, and why, since he did permit it, should he conceal his knowledge of it rom Oliver? And what, oh, what wondrous specific had the mighty man found for his disease?

Morning failed to clarify these mysteries; it brought, however, something rare and rich and strange. I allude to the manner of Amédée's approach. The aged gossip-demoniac had to recognise the fact that he could not keep out of my way for ever; there was nothing for it but to put as good a face as possible upon a bad business, and get it over—and the face he selected was a marvel; not less, and in no hasty sense of the word.

It appeared at my door to announce that breakfast waited outside.

Primarily it displayed an expression of serenity, masterly in its assumption that not the least, remotest, dreamiest shadow of danger could possibly be conceived, by the most immoderately pessimistic and sinister imagination, as even vaguely threatening. And for the rest, you have seen a happy young mother teaching first steps to the first-born—that was Amédée. Radiantly tender, aggressively solicitous, diffusing ineffable sweetness on the air, wreathed in seraphic smiles, beaming caressingly, and aglow with a sacred joy that I should be looking so well, he greeted me in a voice of honey and bowed me to my repast with an unconcealed fondness at once maternal and reverential.

I did not attempt to speak. I came out silently, uncannily fascinated, my eyes fixed upon him, while he moved gently backward, cooing pleasant words about the coffee, but just perceptibly keeping himself out of arm's reach until I had taken my seat. When I had done that, he leaned over the table and began to set useless things nearer my plate with frankly affectionate care. It chanced that in "making a long arm" to reach something I did want, my hand (of which the fingers happened to be closed) passed rather impatiently beneath his nose. The madonna expression changed instantly to one of horror, he uttered a startled croak, and took a surprisingly long skip backward, landing in the screen of honeysuckle vines, which, he seemed to imagine, were some new form of hostility attacking him treacherously from the rear. They sagged, but did not break from their fastenings, and his behaviour, as he lay thus entangled, would have contrasted unfavourably in dignity with the actions of a panicstricken hen in a hammock.

"And so conscience *does* make cowards of us all," I said, with no hope of being understood.

Recovering some measure of mental equilibrium at the same time that he managed to find his feet, he burst into shrill laughter, to which he tried in vain to impart a ring of debonair carelessness.

"Eh, I stumble!" he cried with hollow merriment. "I fall about and faint with fatigue! Pah! But it is nothing; truly!"

"Fatigue!" I turned a bitter sneer upon him. "Fatigue! And you just out of bed!"

His fat hands went up palm outward; his heroic laughter was checked as with a sob; an expression of tragic incredulity shone from his eyes. Patently he doubted the evidence of his own ears; could not believe that such black ingratitude existed in the world. "Absalom, O my son Absalom!" was his unuttered cry. His hands fell to his sides; his chin sank wretchedly into its own folds; his shirt-bosom heaved and crinkled; arrows of unspeakable injustice had entered the defenceless breast.

"Just out of bed!" he repeated, with a pathos that would have brought the judge of any court in France down from the bench to kiss him—"And I had risen long, long before the dawn, in the cold and darkness of the night, to prepare the sandwiches of monsieur!"

It was too much for me, or rather, he was. I stalked off to the woods in a state of helpless indignation; mentally swearing that his day of punishment at my hands was only deferred, not abandoned, yet secretly fearing that this very oath might live for no purpose but to convict me of perjury. His talents were lost in the country; he should have sought his fortune in the metropolis. And his manner, as he summoned me that evening to

dinner, and indeed throughout the courses, partook
of the subtle condescension and careless assurance
of one who has but faintly enjoyed some too easy
triumph.

I found this so irksome that I might have been
goaded into an outbreak of impotent fury, had my
attention not been distracted by the curious turn of
the professor's malady, which had renewed its painful assault upon him. He came hobbling to table,
leaning upon Saffren's shoulder, and made no reference to his singular improvement of the night
before—nor did I. His rheumatism was his own;
he might do what he pleased with it! There was
no reason why he should confide the cause of its
vagaries to me.

Table-talk ran its normal course; a great Pole's
philosophy receiving flagellation at the hands of
our incorrigible optimist. ("If he could understand," exclaimed Keredec, "that the individual
must be immortal before it is born, ha! then this
babbler might have writted some intelligence!")
On the surface everything was as usual with our
trio, with nothing to show any turbulence of under-
currents, unless it was a certain alertness in Oliver's
manner, a restrained excitement, and the question-

ing restlessness of his eyes as they sought mine from time to time. Whatever he wished to ask me, he was given no opportunity, for the professor carried him off to work when our coffee was finished. As they departed, the young man glanced back at me over his shoulder, with that same earnest look of interrogation, but it went unanswered by any token or gesture: for though I guessed that he wished to know if Mrs. Harman had spoken of him to me, it seemed part of my bargain with her to give him no sign that I understood.

A note lay beside my plate next morning, addressed in a writing strange to me, one of dashing and vigorous character.

"In the pursuit of thrillingly scientific research," it read, "what with the tumult which possessed me, I forgot to mention the bond that links us; I, too, am a painter, though as yet unhonoured and unhung. It must be only because I lack a gentle hand to guide me. If I might sit beside you as you paint! The hours pass on leaden wings at Quesnay—I could shriek! Do not refuse me a few words of instruction, either in the wildwood, whither I could support your shrinking steps, or, from time to time, as you work in your studio, which (I glean from the instructive Mr. Ferret) is at *Les Trois Pigeons*. At any hour, at any moment, I will speed to you. I am, sir,

"Yours, if you will but breathe a 'yes,'

"ANNE ELLIOTT."

To this I returned a reply, as much in her own key as I could write it, putting my refusal on the ground that I was not at present painting in the studio. I added that I hoped her suit might prosper, regretting that I could not be of greater assistance to that end, and concluded with the suggestion that Madame Brossard might entertain an offer for lessons in cooking.

The result of my attempt to echo her vivacity was discomfiting, and I was allowed to perceive that epistolary jocularity was not thought to be my line. It was Miss Elizabeth who gave me this instruction three days later, on the way to Quesnay for "second breakfast." Exercising fairly shame-faced diplomacy, I had avoided dining at the château again, but, by arrangement, she had driven over for me this morning in the phaeton.

"Why are you writing silly notes to that child?"

she demanded, as soon as we were away from the inn.

"Was it silly?"

"You should know. Do you think that style of humour suitable for a young girl?"

This bewildered me a little. "But there wasn't anything offensive——"

"No?" Miss Elizabeth lifted her eyebrows to a height of bland inquiry. "She mightn't think it rather—well, rough? Your suggesting that she should take cooking lessons?"

"But *she* suggested she might take *painting* lessons," was my feeble protest. "I only meant to show her I understood that she wanted to get to the inn."

"And why should she care to 'get to the inn'?"

"She seemed interested in a young man who is staying there. 'Interested' is the mildest word for it I can think of."

"Pooh!" Such was Miss Ward's enigmatic retort, and though I begged an explanation I got none. Instead, she quickened the horse's gait and changed the subject.

At the château, having a mind to offer some sort of apology, I looked anxiously about for the subject of our rather disquieting conversation, but she was not to be seen until the party assembled at the table, set under an awning on the terrace. Then, to my disappointment, I found no opportunity to speak to her, for her seat was so placed as to make it impossible, and she escaped into the house immediately upon the conclusion of the repast, hurrying away too pointedly for any attempt to detain her—though, as she passed, she sent me one glance of meek reproach which she was at pains to make elaborately distinct.

Again taking me for her neighbour at the table, Miss Elizabeth talked to me at intervals, apparently having nothing, just then, to make up to Mr. Cresson Ingle, but not long after we rose she accompanied him upon some excursion of an indefinite nature, which led her from my sight. Thus, the others making off to cards indoors and what not, I was left to the perusal of the eighteenth century façade of the château, one of the most competent restorations in that part of France, and of the liveliest interest to the student or practitioner of architecture.

Mrs. Harman had not appeared at all, having gone to call upon some one at Dives, I was told,

and a servant informing me (on inquiry) that Miss
Elliott had retired to her room, I was thrust upon
my own devices indeed, a condition already closely
associated in my mind with this picturesque spot.
The likeliest of my devices—or, at least, the one I
hit upon—was in the nature of an unostentatious
retreat.

I went home.

However, as the day was spoiled for work, I chose
a roundabout way, in fact the longest, and took
the high-road to Dives, but neither the road nor
the town itself (when I passed through it) rewarded
my vague hope that I might meet Mrs. Harman,
and I strode the long miles in considerable dis-
gruntlement, for it was largely in that hope that
I had gone to Quesnay. It put me in no merrier
mood to find Miss Elizabeth's phaeton standing
outside the inn in charge of a groom, for my vanity
encouraged the supposition that she had come out
of a fear that my unceremonious departure from
Quesnay might have indicated that I was "hurt,"
or considered myself neglected; and I dreaded having
to make explanations.

My apprehensions were unfounded; it was not
Miss Elizabeth who had come in the phaeton,

though a lady from Quesnay did prove to be the
occupant—the sole occupant—of the courtyard.
At sight of her I halted stock-still under the
archway.

There she sat, a sketch-book on a green table
beside her and a board in her lap, brazenly painting—and a more blushless piece of assurance than
Miss Anne Elliott thus engaged these eyes have
never beheld.

She was not so hardened that she did not affect
a little timidity at sight of me, looking away even
more quickly than she looked up, while I walked
slowly over to her and took the garden chair beside
her. That gave me a view of her sketch, which
was a violent little "lay-in" of shrubbery, trees,
and the sky-line of the inn. To my prodigious
surprise (and, naturally enough, with a degree of
pleasure) I perceived that it was not very bad,
not bad at all, indeed. It displayed a sense of
values, of placing, and even, in a young and frantic
way, of colour. Here was a young woman of more
than "accomplishments!"

"You see," she said, squeezing one of the tiny
tubes almost dry, and continuing to paint with a
fine effect of absorption, "I *had* to show you that

I was in the most *abysmal* earnest. Will you take me painting with you?"

"I appreciate your seriousness," I rejoined. "Has it been rewarded?"

"How can I say? You haven't told me whether or no I may follow you to the wildwood."

"I mean, have you caught another glimpse of Mr. Saffren?"

At that she showed a prettier colour in her cheeks than any in her sketch-box, but gave no other sign of shame, nor even of being flustered, cheerfully replying:

"That is far from the point. Do you grant my burning plea?"

"I understood I had offended you."

"You did," she said. *"Viciously!"*

"I am sorry," I continued. "I wanted to ask you to forgive me——"

I spoke seriously, and that seemed to strike her as odd or needing explanation, for she levelled her blue eyes at me, and interrupted, with something more like seriousness in her own voice than I had yet heard from her:

"What made you think I was offended?"

"Your look of reproach when you left the table——"

"Nothing else?" she asked quickly.

"Yes; Miss Ward told me you were."

"Yes; she drove over with you. That's it!" she exclaimed with vigour, and nodded her head as if some suspicion of hers had been confirmed. "I thought so!"

"You thought she had told me?"

"No," said Miss Elliott decidedly. "Thought that Elizabeth wanted to have her cake and eat it too."

"I don't understand."

"Then you'll get no help from me," she returned slowly, a frown marking her pretty forehead. "But I was only playing offended, and she knew it. I thought your note was *that* fetching!"

She continued to look thoughtful for a moment longer, then with a resumption of her former manner —the pretence of an earnestness much deeper than the real—"Will you take me painting with you?" she said. "If it will convince you that I mean it, I'll give up my hopes of seeing that *sumptuous* Mr. Saffren and go back to Quesnay now, before he comes home. He's been out for a walk—a long one, since it's lasted ever since early this morning, so the waiter told me. May I go with you? You *can't* know how enervating it is up there at the château—all except Mrs. Harman, and even she——"

"What about Mrs. Harman?" I asked, as she paused.

"I think she must be in love."

"What!"

"I do think so," said the girl. "She's *like* it, at least."

"But with whom?"

She laughed gaily. "I'm afraid she's my rival!"

"Not with——" I began.

"Yes, with your beautiful and mad young friend."

"But—oh, it's preposterous!" I cried, profoundly disturbed. "She couldn't be! If you knew a great deal about her——"

"I may know more than you think. My simplicity of appearance is deceptive," she mocked, beginning to set her sketch-box in order. "You don't realise that Mrs. Harman and I are quite *hurled* upon each other at Quesnay, being two ravishingly intelligent women entirely surrounded by large bodies of elementals. She has told me a great deal of herself since that first evening, and I know—well, I know why she did not come back from Dives this afternoon, for instance."

"*Why?*" I fairly shouted.

She slid her sketch into a groove in the box, which she closed, and rose to her feet before answering. Then she set her hat a little straighter with a touch, looking so fixedly and with such grave interest over my shoulder that I turned to follow her glance and encountered our reflections in a window of the inn. Her own shed a light upon *that* mystery, at all events.

"I might tell you some day," she said indifferently, "if I gained enough confidence in you through association in daily pursuits."

"My dear young lady," I cried with real exasperation, "I am a working man, and this is a working summer for me!"

"Do you think I'd spoil it?" she urged gently.

"But I get up with the first daylight to paint," I protested, "and I paint all day——"

She moved a step nearer me and laid her hand warningly upon my sleeve, checking the outburst.

I turned to see what she meant.

Oliver Saffren had come in from the road and was crossing to the gallery steps. He lifted his hat and gave me a quick word of greeting as he passed, and at the sight of his flushed and happy face my riddle was solved for me. Amazing as the thing was, I had no doubt of the revelation.

"Ah," I said to Miss Elliott when he had gone, "I won't have to take pupils to get the answer to my question, now!"

CHAPTER XIV

H A, these philosophers," said the professor,
expanding in discourse a little later—
"these dreamy people who talk of the
spirit, they tell you that spirit is abstract!" He
waved his great hand in a sweeping semicircle
which carried it out of our orange candle-light
and freckled it with the cold moonshine which
sieved through the loosened screen of honeysuckle.
"Ha, the folly!"

"What do *you* say it is?" I asked, moving so that
the smoke of my cigar should not drift toward Oliver,
who sat looking out into the garden.

"I, my friend? I do not say that it *is!* But all
such things, they are only a question of names, and
when I use the word 'spirit' I mean identity—
universal identity, if you like. It is what we all
are, yes—and those flowers, too. But the spirit of
the flowers is not what you smell, nor what you
see, that look so pretty: it is the flowers themself!
Yet all spirit is only one spirit and one spirit is all

spirit—and if you tell me this is Pant'eism I will tell you that you do not understand!"

"I don't tell you that," said I, "neither do I understand."

"Nor that big Keredec either!" Whereupon he loosed the rolling thunder of his laughter. "Nor any brain born of the monkey people! But this world is full of proof that everything that exist is all one thing, and it is the instinct of that, when it draws us together, which makes what we call 'love.' Even those wicked devils of egoism in our inside is only love which grows too long the wrong way, like the finger nails of the Chinese empress. Young love is a little sprout of universal unity. When the young people begin to feel it, *they* are not abstract, ha? And the young man, when he selects, he chooses one being from all the others to mean—just for him—all that great universe of which he is a part."

This was wandering whimsically far afield, but as I caught the good-humoured flicker of the professor's glance at our companion I thought I saw a purpose in his deviation. Saffren turned toward him wonderingly, his unconscious, eager look remarkably emphasised and brightened.

"All such things are most strange—great mysteries," continued the professor. "For when a man has made the selection, *that* being *does* become all the universe, and for him there is nothing else at all—nothing else anywhere!"

Saffren's cheeks and temples were flushed as they had been when I saw him returning that afternoon; and his eyes were wide, fixed upon Keredec in a stare of utter amazement.

"Yes, that is true," he said slowly. "How did you know?"

Keredec returned his look with an attentive scrutiny, and made some exclamation under his breath, which I did not catch, but there was no mistaking his high good humour.

"Bravo!" he shouted, rising and clapping the other upon the shoulder. "You will soon cure my rheumatism if you ask me questions like that! Ho, ho, ho!" He threw back his head and let the mighty salvos forth. "Ho, ho, ho! How do I know? The young, always they believe they are the only ones who were ever young! Ho, ho, ho! Come, we shall make those lessons very easy to-night. Come, my friend! How could that big, old Keredec know of such things? He is too old, too foolish! Ho, ho, ho!"

As he went up the steps, the courtyard rever-
berating again to his laughter, his arm resting
on Saffren's shoulders, but not so heavily as usual.
The door of their salon closed upon them, and for
a while Keredec's voice could be heard boom-
ing cheerfully; it ended in another burst of
laughter.

A moment later Saffren opened the door and
called to me.

"Here," I answered from my veranda, where I
had just lighted my second cigar.

"No more work to-night. All finished," he cried
jubilantly, springing down the steps. "I'm coming
to have a talk with you."

Amédée had removed the candles, the moon had
withdrawn in fear of a turbulent mob of clouds,
rioting into our sky from seaward; the air smelled
of imminent rain, and it was so dark that I could
see my visitor only as a vague, tall shape; but a
happy excitement vibrated in his rich voice, and
his step on the gravelled path was light and
exultant.

"I won't sit down," he said. "I'll walk up and
down in front of the veranda—if it doesn't make
you nervous."

For answer I merely laughed; and he laughed too, in genial response, continuing gaily:

"Oh, it's all so different with me! Everything is. That *blind* feeling I told you of—it's all gone. I must have been very babyish, the other day; I don't think I could feel like that again. It used to seem to me that I lived penned up in a circle of blank stone walls; I couldn't see over the top for myself at all, though now and then Keredec would boost me up and let me get a little glimmer of the country round about—but never long enough to see what it was really like. But it's not so now. Ah!"—he drew a long breath—"I'd like to run. I think I could run all the way to the top of a pretty fair-sized mountain to-night, and then"—he laughed—"jump off and ride on the clouds."

"I know how that is," I responded. "At least I did know—a few years ago."

"Everything is a jumble with me," he went on happily, in a confidential tone, "yet it's a heavenly kind of jumble. I can't put anything into words. I don't *think* very well yet, though Keredec is trying to teach me. My thoughts don't run in order, and this that's happened seems to make them wilder, queerer—" He stopped short.

"What has happened?"

He paused in his sentry-go, facing me, and answered, in a low voice:

"I've seen her again."

"Yes, I know."

"She told me you knew it," he said, "—that she had told you."

"Yes."

"But that's not all," he said, his voice rising a little. "I saw her again the day after she told you——"

"You did!" I murmured.

"Oh, I tell myself that it's a dream," he cried, "that it *can't* be true. For it has been *every* day since then! That's why I haven't joined you in the woods. I have been with her, walking with her, listening to her, looking at her—always feeling that it must be unreal and that I must try not to wake up. She has been so kind—so wonderfully, beautifully kind to me!"

"She has met you?" I asked, thinking ruefully of George Ward, now on the high seas in the pleasant company of old hopes renewed.

"She has let me meet her. And to-day we lunched at the inn at Dives and then walked by the sea all

afternoon. She gave me the whole day—the whole
day! You see"—he began to pace again—"you see
I was right, and you were wrong. She wasn't
offended—she was glad—that I couldn't help speaking to her; she has said so."

"Do you think," I interrupted, "that she would
wish you to tell me this?"

"Ah, she likes you!" he said so heartily, and
appearing meanwhile so satisfied with the com-
pleteness of his reply, that I was fain to take some
satisfaction in it myself. "What I wanted most to
say to you," he went on, "is this: you remember
you promised to tell me whatever you could learn
about her—and about her husband?"

"I remember."

"It's different now. I don't want you to," he said.
"I want only to know what she tells me herself. She
has told me very little, but I know when the time comes
she *will* tell me everything. But I wouldn't hasten
it. I wouldn't have anything changed from just *this!*"

"You mean——"

"I mean the way it *is*. If I could hope to see her
every day, to be in the woods with her, or down by
the shore—oh, I don't want to know anything but
that!"

"No doubt you have told her," I ventured, "a good deal about yourself," and was instantly ashamed of myself. I suppose I spoke out of a sense of protest against Mrs. Harman's strange lack of conventionality, against so charming a lady's losing her head as completely as she seemed to have lost hers, and it may have been, too, out of a feeling of jealousy for poor George—possibly even out of a little feeling of the same sort on my own account. But I couldn't have said it except for the darkness, and, as I say, I was instantly ashamed.

It does not whiten my guilt that the shaft did not reach him.

"I've told her all I know," he said readily, and the unconscious pathos of the answer smote me. "And all that Keredec has let me know. You see I haven't——"

"But do you think," I interrupted quickly, anxious, in my remorse, to divert him from that channel, "do you think Professor Keredec would approve, if he knew?"

"I think he would," he responded slowly, pausing in his walk again. "I have a feeling that perhaps he does know, and yet I have been afraid to tell him,

afraid he might try to stop me—keep me from
going to wait for her. But he has a strange way
of knowing things; I think he knows everything in
the world! I have felt to-night that he knows this,
and—it's very strange, but I—well, what *was* it
that made him so glad?"

"The light is still burning in his room," I said
quietly.

"You mean that I ought to tell him?" His voice
rose a little.

"He's done a good deal for you, hasn't he?" I
suggested. "And even if he does know he might
like to hear it from you."

"You're right; I'll tell him to-night." This came
with sudden decision, but with less than marked
what followed. "But he can't stop me, now. No
one on earth shall do that, except Madame d'Armand herself. No one!"

"I won't quarrel with that," I said drily, throwing away my cigar, which had gone out long before.

He hesitated, and then I saw his hand groping
toward me in the darkness, and, rising, I gave him
mine.

"Good night," he said, and shook my hand as the
first sputterings of the coming rain began to patter

on the roof of the pavilion. "I'm glad to tell him; I'm glad to have told you. Ah, but isn't this," he cried, "a happy world!"

Turning, he ran to the gallery steps. "At last I'm glad," he called back over his shoulder, "I'm glad that I was born——"

A gust of wind blew furiously into the courtyard at that instant, and I heard his voice indistinctly, but I thought—though I might have been mistaken —that I caught a final word, and that it was "again."

CHAPTER XV

THE rain of two nights and two days had freshened the woods, deepening the green of the tree-trunks and washing the dust from the leaves, and now, under the splendid sun of the third morning, we sat painting in a sylvan aisle that was like a hall of Aladdin's palace, the filigreed arches of foliage above us glittering with pendulous rain-drops. But Arabian Nights' palaces are not to my fancy for painting; the air, rinsed of its colour, was too sparklingly clean; the interstices of sky and the roughly framed distances I prized, were brought too close. It was one of those days when Nature throws herself straight in your face and you are at a loss to know whether she has kissed you or slapped you, though you are conscious of the tingle; —a day, in brief, more for laughing than for painting, and the truth is that I suited its mood only too well, and laughed more than I painted, though I sat with my easel before me and a picture ready upon my palette to be painted.

No one could have understood better than I that

this was setting a bad example to the acolyte who
sat, likewise facing an easel, ten paces to my left; a
very sportsmanlike figure of a painter indeed, in her
short skirt and long coat of woodland brown, the
fine brown of dead oak-leaves; a "devastating"
selection of colour that!—being much the same
shade as her hair—with brown for her hat too,
and the veil encircling the small crown thereof,
and brown again for the stout, high, laced boots
which protected her from the wet tangle underfoot. Who could have expected so dashing a young
person as this to do any real work at painting?
Yet she did, narrowing her eyes to the finest point
of concentration, and applying herself to the task
in hand with a persistence which I found, on that
particular morning, far beyond my own powers.

As she leaned back critically, at the imminent
risk of capsizing her camp-stool, and herself with
it, in her absorption, some ill-suppressed token of
amusement most have caught her ear, for she turned
upon me with suspicion, and was instantly moved
to moralize upon the reluctance I had shown to
accept her as a companion for my excursions; taking
as her theme, in contrast, her own present display
of ambition; all in all a warm, if overcoloured,

sketch of the idle master and the industrious apprentice. It made me laugh again, upon which she changed the subject.

"An indefinable something tells me," she announced coldly, "that henceforth you needn't be so *drastically* fearful of being dragged to the château for dinner, nor *dejéuner* either!"

"Did anything ever tell you that I had cause to fear it?"

"Yes," she said, but too simply. "Jean Ferret."

"Anglicise that ruffian's name," I muttered, mirth immediately withering upon me, "and you'll know him better. To save time: will you mention anything you can think of that he *hasn't* told you?"

Miss Elliott cocked her head upon one side to examine the work of art she was producing, while a slight smile, playing about her lips, seemed to indicate that she was appeased. "You and Miss Ward are old and dear friends, aren't you?" she asked absently.

"We are!" I answered between my teeth. "For years I have sent her costly jewels——"

She interrupted me by breaking outright into a peal of laughter, which rang with such childish delight that I retorted by offering several malevolent

"You and Miss Ward are old and very dear friends, aren't you?"

observations upon the babbling of French servants and the order of mind attributable to those who listened to them. Her defence was to affect inattention and paint busily until some time after I had concluded.

"I think she's going to take Cressie Ingle," she said dreamily, with the air of one whose thoughts have been far, far away. "It looks preponderously like it. She's been teetertottering these *ages* and ages between you——"

"Between whom?"

"You and Mr. Ingle," she replied, not altering her tone in the slightest. "But she's all for her brother, of course, and though you're his friend, Ingle is a personage in the world they court, and among the *multitudinous* things his father left him is an art magazine, or one that's long on art or something of that sort—I don't know just what—so altogether it will be a good thing for *dearest* Mr. Ward. She likes Cressie, of course, though I think she likes you better——"

I managed to find my voice and interrupt the thistle-brained creature. "What put these fantasias into your head?"

"Not Jean Ferret," she responded promptly.

"It's cruel of me to break it to you so coarsely—
I know—but if you are ever going to make up
your mind to her building as glaring a success
of you as she has of her brother, I think you must
do it now. She's on the point of accepting Mr.
Ingle, and what becomes of *you* will depend on
your conduct in the most immediate future. She
won't ask you to Quesnay again, so you'd better
go up there on your own accord.—And on your
bended knees, too!" she added as an afterthought.

I sought for something to say which might have
a chance of impressing her—a desperate task on the
face of it—and I mentioned that Miss Ward was
her hostess.

One might as well have tried to impress Amédée.
She "made a little mouth" and went on dabbling
with her brushes. "Hostess? Pooh!" she said
cheerfully. "My *infantile* father sent me here to
be in her charge while he ran home to America.
Mr. Ward's to paint my portrait, when he comes.
Give and take—it's simple enough, you see!"

Here was frankness with a vengeance, and I fell
back upon silence, whereupon a pause ensued, to
my share of which I imparted the deepest shadow
of disapproval within my power. Unfortunately,

she did not look at me; my effort passed with no other effect than to make some of my facial muscles ache.

" 'Portrait of Miss E., by George Ward, H. C.,' " this painfully plain-speaking young lady continued presently. "On the line at next spring's Salon, then packed up for the dear ones at home. I'd as soon own an 'Art Bronze,' myself—or a nice, clean porcelain Arab."

"No doubt you've forgotten for the moment," I said, "that Mr. Ward is my friend."

"Not in painting, he isn't," she returned quickly.

"I consider his work altogether creditable; it's carefully done, conscientious, effective——"

"Isn't that true of the ladies in the hairdressers' windows?" she asked with assumed artlessness. "Can't you say a kind word for them, good gentleman, and heaven bless you?"

"Why sha'n't I be asked to Quesnay again?"

She laughed. "You haven't seemed *fanatically* appreciative of your opportunities when you have been there; you might have carried her off from Cresson Ingle instead of vice versa. But after all, you *aren't*"—here she paused and looked at me appraisingly for a moment—"you *aren't* the most piratical dash-in-and-dash-out and leave-every-thing-upside-down-behind-you sort of man, are you?"

"No, I believe I'm not."

"However, that's only a *small* half of the reason," Miss Elliott went on. "She's furious on account of this."

These were vague words, and I said so.

"Oh, *this*," she explained, "my being here; your letting me come. Impropriety—all of that!" A sharp whistle issued from her lips. "Oh! the *excoriating* things she's said of my pursuing you!"

"But doesn't she know that it's only part of your siege of Madame Brossard's; that it's a subterfuge in the hope of catching a glimpse of Oliver Saffren?"

"No!" she cried, her eyes dancing; "I told her that, but she thinks it's only a subterfuge in the hope of catching more than a glimpse of you!"

I joined laughter with her then. She was the first to stop, and, looking at me somewhat doubt-fully, she said:

"Whereas, the truth is that it's neither. You know very well that I want to paint."

"Certainly," I agreed at once. "Your devotion to 'your art' and your hope of spending half an hour at Madame Brossard's now and then are separable;—which reminds me: Wouldn't you like me to look at your sketch?"

"No, not yet." She jumped up and brought her camp-stool over to mine. "I feel that I could better bear what you'll say of it after I've had some lunch. Not a *syllable* of food has crossed my lips since coffee at dawn!"

I spread before her what Amédée had prepared; not sandwiches for the pocket to-day, but a wicker hamper, one end of which we let rest upon her knees, the other upon mine, and at sight of the *foie gras*, the delicate, devilled partridge, the truffled salad, the fine yellow cheese, and the long bottle of good red Beaune, revealed when the cover was off, I could almost have forgiven the old rascal for his scandal-mongering. As for my vis-á-vis, she pronounced it a "maddening sight."

"Fall to, my merry man," she added, "and eat your fill of this fair pasty, under the greenwood tree." Obeying her instructions with right good-will, and the lady likewise evincing no hatred of the viands, we made a cheerful meal of it, topping it with peaches and bunches of grapes.

"It is unfair to let you do all the catering,"

said Miss Elliott, after carefully selecting the largest and best peach.

"Jean Ferret's friend does that," I returned, watching her rather intently as she dexterously peeled the peach. She did it very daintily, I had to admit that—though I regretted to observe indications of the gourmet in one so young. But when it was peeled clean, she set it on a fresh green leaf, and, to my surprise, gave it to me.

"You see," she continued, not observing my remorseful confusion, "I couldn't destroy Elizabeth's peace of mind and then raid her larder to boot. That poor lady! I make her trouble enough, but it's nothing to what she's going to have when she finds out some things that she must find out."

"What is that?"

"About Mrs. Harman," was the serious reply. "Elizabeth hasn't a clue."

" 'Clue'?" I echoed.

"To Louise's strange affair." Miss Elliott's expression had grown as serious as her tone. "It is strange; the strangest thing I ever knew."

"But there's your own case," I urged. "Why should you think it strange of her to take an interest in Saffren?"

"I adore him, of course," she said. "He is the most glorious-looking person I've ever seen, but on my *word*—" She paused, and as her gaze met mine I saw real earnestness in her eyes. "I'm afraid—I was half joking the other day—but now I'm really afraid Louise is beginning to be in love with him."

"Oh, mightn't it be only interest, so far?" I said.

"No, it's much more. And I've grown so fond of her!" the girl went on, her voice unexpectedly verging upon tremulousness. "She's quite wonder·ful in her way—such an understanding sort of woman, and generous and kind; there are so many things turning up in a party like ours at Quesnay that show what people are really made of, and she's a rare, fine spirit. It seems a pity, with such a miserable first experience as she had, that this should happen. Oh I know," she continued rapidly, cutting off a half-formed protest of mine. "He isn't mad—and I'm sorry I tried to be amusing about it the night you dined at the château. I know perfectly well he's not insane; but I'm absolutely sure, from one thing and another, that— well—he isn't *all there!* He's as beautiful as a seraph and probably as good as one, but something is *missing* about him—and it begins to look like a second tragedy for her."

"You mean, she really—" I began.

"Yes, I do," she returned, with a catch in her throat. "She comes to my room when the others are asleep. Not that she tells me a great deal, but it's in the air, somehow; she told me with such a strained sort of gaiety of their meeting and his first joining her; and there was something underneath as if she thought *I* might be really serious in my ravings about him, and—yes, as if she meant to warn me off. And the other night, when I saw her after their lunching together at Dives, I asked her teasingly if she'd had a happy day, and she laughed the prettiest laugh I ever heard and put her arms around me—then suddenly broke out crying and ran out of the room."

"But that may have been no more than over-strained nerves," I feebly suggested.

"Of course it was!" she cried, regarding me with justifiable astonishment. "It's the *cause* of their being overstrained that interests me! It's all so strange and distressing," she continued more gently, "that I wish I weren't there to see it. And there's poor George Ward coming—ah! and when Elizabeth learns of it!"

"Mrs. Harman had her way once, in spite of everything," I said thoughtfully.

"Yes, she was a headstrong girl of nineteen, then. But let's not think it could go as far as that! There!" She threw a peach-stone over her shoulder and sprang up gaily. "Let's not talk of it; I *think* of it enough! It's time for you to give me a *racking* criticism on my morning's work."

Taking off her coat as she spoke, she unbuttoned the cuffs of her manly blouse and rolled up her sleeves as far as they would go, preparations which I observed with some perplexity.

"If you intend any violence," said I, "in case my views of your work shouldn't meet your own, I think I'll be leaving."

"Wait," she responded, and kneeling upon one knee beside a bush near by, thrust her arms elbow-deep under the outer mantle of leaves, shaking the stems vigorously, and sending down a shower of sparkling drops. Never lived sane man, or madman, since time began, who, seeing her then, could or would have denied that she made the very prettiest picture ever seen by any person or persons whatsoever—but her purpose was difficult to fathom. Pursuing it, I remarked that it was improbable that birds would be nesting so low.

"It's for a finger bowl," she said briskly. And rising, this most practical of her sex dried her hands upon a fresh serviette from the hamper. "Last night's rain is worth two birds in the bush."

With that, she readjusted her sleeves, lightly donned her coat, and preceded me to her easel. "Now," she commanded, "slaughter! It's what I let you come with me for."

I looked at her sketch with much more attention than I had given the small board she had used as a bait in the courtyard of *Les Trois Pigeons*. To-day she showed a larger ambition, and a larger canvas as well—or, perhaps I should say a larger burlap, for she had chosen to paint upon something strongly resembling a square of coffee-sacking. But there was no doubt she had "found colour" in a swash-buckling, bullying style of forcing it to be there, whether it was or not, and to "vibrate," whether it did or not. There was not much to be said, for the violent kind of thing she had done always hushes me; and even when it is well done I am never sure whether its right place is the "Salon des Independants" or the Luxembourg. It *seems* dreadful, and yet sometimes I fear in secret that it may be a real transition, or even an awakening, and that the men I began with, and I, are standing still. The older men called *us* lunatics once, and the critics said we were "daring," but that was long ago.

"Well?" she said.

I had to speak, so I paraphrased a *mot* of Degas (I think it was Degas) and said:

"If Rousseau could come to life and see this sketch of yours, I imagine he would be very much interested, but if he saw mine he might say, 'That is my fault!' "

"*Oh!*" she cried, her colour rising quickly; she looked troubled for a second, then her eyes twinkled. "You're not going to let my work make a difference between us, are you?"

"I'll even try to look at it from your own point of view," I answered, stepping back several yards to see it better, though I should have had to retire about a quarter of the length of a city block to see it quite from her own point of view.

She moved with me, both of us walking backward. I began:

"For a day like this, with all the colour in the trees themselves and so very little in the air——"

There came an interruption, a voice of unpleasant and wiry nasality, speaking from behind us.

"*Well, well!*" it said. "So here we are again!"

I faced about and beheld, just emerged from a by-path, a fox-faced young man whose light, well-poised figure was jauntily clad in gray serge, with scarlet waistcoat and tie, white shoes upon his feet, and a white hat, gaily beribboned, upon his head. A recollection of the dusky road and a group of people about Père Baudry's lamplit door flickered across my mind.

"The historical tourist!" I exclaimed. "The highly pedestrian tripper from Trouville!"

"You got me right, m'dear friend," he replied with condescension; "I rec'leck meetin' you perfect."

"And I was interested to learn," said I, carefully observing the effect of my words upon him, "that you had been to *Les Trois Pigeons* after all. Perhaps I might put it, you had been through *Les Trois Pigeons*, for the *maître d'hôtel* informed me you had investigated every corner—that wasn't locked."

"Sure," he returned, with rather less embarrassment than a brazen Vishnu would have exhibited under the same circumstances. "He showed me what pitchers they was in your studio. I'll luk 'em over again fer ye one of these days. Some of 'em was right gud."

"You will be visiting near enough for me to avail myself of the opportunity?"

"Right in the Pigeon House, m'friend. I've just come down t'putt in a few days there," he responded coolly. "They's a young feller in this neighbourhood I take a kind o' fam'ly interest in."

"Who is that?" I asked quickly.

For answer he produced the effect of a laugh by widening and lifting one side of his mouth, leaving the other, meantime, rigid.

"Don' lemme int'rup' the conv'sation with yer lady-friend," he said winningly. "What they call 'talkin' High Arts,' wasn't it? I'd like to hear some."

CHAPTER XVI

MISS ELLIOTT'S expression, when I turned to observe the effect of the intruder upon her, was found to be one of brilliant delight. With glowing eyes, her lips parted in a breathless ecstasy, she gazed upon the new-comer, evidently fearing to lose a syllable that fell from his lips. Moving closer to me she whispered urgently:

"Keep him. Oh, keep him!"

To detain him, for a time at least, was my intention, though my motive was not merely to afford her pleasure. The advent of the young man had produced a singularly disagreeable impression upon me, quite apart from any antagonism I might have felt toward him as a type. Strange suspicions leaped into my mind, formless—in the surprise of the moment—but rapidly groping toward definite outline; and following hard upon them crept a tingling apprehension. The reappearance of this rattish youth, casual as was the air with which he strove to invest it, began to assume, for me, the character

212

of a theatrical entrance of unpleasant portent—a suggestion just now enhanced by an absurdly obvious notion of his own that he was enacting a part. This was written all over him, most legibly in his attitude of the knowing amateur, as he surveyed Miss Elliott's painting patronisingly, his head on one side, his cane in the crook of his elbows behind his back, and his body teetering genteelly as he shifted his weight from his toes to his heels and back again, nodding meanwhile a slight but judicial approbation.

"Now, about how much," he said slowly, "would you expec' t' git f'r a pitcher that size?"

"It isn't mine," I informed him.

"You don't tell me it's the little lady's—what?" He bowed genially and favoured Miss Elliott with a stare of warm admiration. "Pretty a thing as I ever see," he added.

"Oh," she cried with an ardour that choked her slightly. "*Thank* you!"

"Oh, I meant the *pitcher!*" he said hastily, evidently nonplussed by a gratitude so fervent.

The incorrigible damsel cast down her eyes in modesty. "And I had hoped," she breathed, "something so different!"

I could not be certain whether or not he caught the whisper; I thought he did. At all events, the surface of his easy assurance appeared somewhat disarranged; and, perhaps to restore it by performing the rites of etiquette, he said:

"Well, I expec' the smart thing now is to pass the cards, but mine's in my grip an' it ain't unpacked yet. The name you'd see on 'em is Oil Poicy."

"Oil Poicy," echoed Miss Elliott, turning to me in genuine astonishment.

"Mr. Earl Percy," I translated.

"Oh, *rapturous!*" she cried, her face radiant. "And *won't* Mr. Percy give us his opinion of my Art?"

Mr. Percy was in doubt how to take her enthusiasm; he seemed on the point of turning surly, and hesitated, while a sharp vertical line appeared on his small forehead; but he evidently concluded, after a deep glance at her, that if she was making game of him it was in no ill-natured spirit—nay, I think that for a few moments he suspected her liveliness to be some method of her own for the incipient stages of a flirtation.

Finally he turned again to the easel, and as he

examined the painting thereon at closer range, amazement overspread his features. However, pulling himself together, he found himself able to reply —and with great gallantry:

"Well, on'y t' think them little hands cud 'a' done all that rough woik!"

The unintended viciousness of this retort produced an effect so marked, that, except for my growing uneasiness, I might have enjoyed her expression.

As it was, I saved her face by entering into the conversation with a question, which I put quickly:

"You intend pursuing your historical researches in the neighborhood?"

The facial contortion which served him for a laugh, and at the same time as a symbol of unfathomable reserve, was repeated, accompanied by a jocose manifestation, in the nature of a sharp and taunting cackle, which seemed to indicate a conviction that he was getting much the best of it in some conflict of wits.

"Them fairy tales I handed you about ole Jeanne d'Arc and William the Conker," he said, "say, they must 'a' made you sore after-*woids!*"

"On the contrary, I was much interested in every-

thing pertaining to your too brief visit," I returned;
"I am even more so now."

"Well, m'friend"—he shot me a sidelong, dis-
trustful glance—"keep yer eyes open."

"That is just the point!" I laughed, with inten-
tional significance, for I meant to make Mr. Percy
talk as much as I could. To this end, remembering that specimens of his kind are most indiscreet
when carefully enraged, I added, simulating his
own manner:

"Eyes open—and doors locked! What?"

At this I heard a gasp of astonishment from Miss
Elliott, who must have been puzzled indeed; but I
was intent upon the other. He proved perfectly
capable of being insulted.

"I guess they ain't much need o' lockin' *your*
door," he retorted darkly; "not from what I saw
when I was in your studio!" He should have stopped
there, for the hit was palpable and justified; but in
his resentment he overdid it. "You needn't be
scared of anybody's cartin' off *them* pitchers, young
feller! *Whoosh!* An' f'm the luks of the *clo'es* I saw
hangin' on the wall," he continued, growing more net-
tled as I smiled cheerfully upon him, "I don' b'lieve
you gut any worries comin' about *them*, neither!"

"I suppose our tastes are different," I said, letting my smile broaden. "There might be protection in that."

His stare at me was protracted to an unseemly length before the sting of this remark reached him; it penetrated finally, however, and in his sharp change of posture there was a lightning flicker of the experienced boxer; but he checked the impulse, and took up the task of obliterating me in another way.

"As I tell the little dame here," he said, pitching his voice higher and affecting the plaintive, "I make no passes at a friend o' her—not in front o' her, anyways. But when it comes to these here ole, ancient curiosities"—he cackled again, loudly—"well, I guess them clo'es I see, that day, kin hand it out t' anything they got in the museums! 'Look here,' I says to the waiter, '*these* must be'n left over f'm ole Jeanne d'Arc herself,' I says. 'Talk about yer relics,' I says. Whoosh! I'd like t' died!" He laughed violently, and concluded by turning upon me with a contemptuous flourish of his stick. "You think I d'know what makes *you* so raw?"

The form of repartee necessary to augment his ill humour was, of course, a matter of simple mechan-

ism for one who had not entirely forgotten his
student days in the Quarter; and I delivered it
airily, though I shivered inwardly that Miss Elliott
should hear.

"Everything will be all right if, when you dine
at the inn, you'll sit with your back toward me."

To my shamed surprise, this roustabout wit drew
a nervous, silvery giggle from her; and that completed the work with Mr. Percy, whose face grew
scarlet with anger.

"You're a hot one, you are!" he sneered, with
shocking bitterness. "You're quite the teaser, ain't
ye, s'long's yer lady-friend is lukkin' on! I guess
they'll be a few surprises comin' *your* way, before
long. P'raps I cudn't give ye one now 'f I had a
mind to."

"Pshaw," I laughed, and, venturing at hazard,
said, "I know all *you* know!"

"Oh, you do!" he cried scornfully. "I reckon
you might set up an' take a little notice, though,
if you knowed 'at I know all *you* know!"

"Not a bit of it!"

"No? Maybe you think I don't know what makes
you so raw with *me?* Maybe you think I don't
know who ye've got so thick with at this here

Pigeon House; maybe you think I don't know who them people *are!*"

"No, you don't. You have learned," I said, trying to control my excitement, "nothing! Whoever hired *you* for a spy lost the money. *You* don't know *any*-thing!"

"I *don't!*" And with that his voice went to a half-shriek. "Maybe you think I'm down here f'r my health; maybe you think I come out f'r a pleasant walk in the woods right now; maybe you think I ain't seen no other lady-friend o' yours besides this'n to-day, and maybe I didn't see who was with her—yes, an' maybe you think I d'know no other times he's be'n with her. Maybe you think I ain't be'n layin' low over at Dives! Maybe I don't know a few real *names* in this neighbourhood! Oh, no, *maybe* not!"

"You know what the maître d'hôtel told you; nothing more."

"How about the name—*Oliver Saffren?*" he cried fiercely, and at last, though I had expected it, I uttered an involuntary exclamation.

"How about it?" he shouted, advancing toward me triumphantly, shaking his forefinger in my face. "Hey? *That* stings some, does it? Sounds kind o'

like a *false* name, does it? Got ye where the hair
is short, that time, didn't I?"

"Speaking of names," I retorted, " 'Oil Poicy'
doesn't seem to ring particularly true to me!"

"It'll be gud enough fer you, young feller," he
responded angrily. "It may belong t' me, an' then
again, it maybe don't. It ain' gunna git me in no
trouble; I'll luk out f'r that. *Your* side's where
the trouble is; that's what's eatin' into you. An'
I'll tell you flat-foot, your gittin' rough 'ith me
and playin' Charley the Show-Off in front o' yer
lady-friends'll all go down in the bill. These people
ye've got so chummy with—*they'll* pay f'r it all
right, don't you shed no tears over that!"

"You couldn't by any possibility," I said deliberately, with as much satire as I could command, "you
couldn't possibly mean that any sum of mere
money might be a salve for the injuries my unkind
words have inflicted?"

Once more he seemed upon the point of destroying
me physically, but, with a slight shudder, controlled
himself. Stepping close to me, he thrust his head
forward and measured the emphases of his speech
by his right forefinger upon my shoulder, as he
said:

CHAPTER SIXTEEN 221

"You paint *this* in yer pitchers, m' dear friend;
they's jest as much law in this country as they is
on the corner o' Twenty-thoid Street an' Fif'
Avenoo! You keep out the way of it, or you'll
git runned over!"

Delivering a final tap on my shoulder as a last
warning, he wheeled deftly upon his heel, addressed
Miss Elliott briefly, "Glad t' know *you*, lady," and
striking into the by-path by which he had approached us, was soon lost to sight.

The girl faced me excitedly. "What *is* it?" she
cried. "It seemed to me you insulted him deliberately——"

"I did."

"You wanted to make him angry?"

"Yes."

"Oh! I thought so!" she exclaimed breathlessly.
"I knew there was something serious underneath.
It's about Mr. Saffren?"

"It is serious indeed, I fear," I said, and turning
to my own easel, began to get my traps together.
"I'll tell you the little I know, because I want you
to tell Mrs. Harman what has just happened, and
you'll be able to do it better if you understand what
is understandable about the rest of it."

"You mean you wouldn't tell me so that I could understand for myself?" There was a note of genuine grieved reproach in her voice. "Ah, then I've made you think me altogether a hare-brain!"

"I haven't time to tell you what I think of you," I said brusquely, and, strangely enough, it seemed to please her. But I paid little attention to that, continuing quickly: "When Professor Keredec and Mr. Saffren came to *Les Trois Pigeons*, they were so careful to keep out of everybody's sight that one might have suspected that they were in hiding —and, in fact, I'm sure that they were—though, as time passed and nothing alarming happened, they've felt reassured and allowed themselves more liberty. It struck me that Keredec at first dreaded that they might be traced to the inn, and I'm afraid his fear was justified, for one night, before I came to know them, I met Mr. 'Percy' on the road; he'd visited Madame Brossard's and pumped Amédée dry, but clumsily tried to pretend to me that he had not been there at all. At the time, I did not connect him even remotely with Professor Keredec's anxieties. I imagined he might have an eye to the spoons; but it's as ridiculous to think him a burglar as it would be to take him for a detective. What he is, or what he has to do with Mr. Saffren, I can guess no more than I can guess the cause of Keredec's fears, but the moment I saw him to-day, saw that he'd come back, I knew it was *that*, and tried to draw him out. You heard what he said; there's no doubt that Saffren stands in danger of some kind. It may be inconsiderable, or even absurd, but it's evidently imminent, and no matter what it is, Mrs. Harman must be kept out of it. I want you to see her as soon as you can and ask her from me—no, persuade her yourself —not to leave Quesnay for a day or two. I mean, that she absolutely *must not* meet Mr. Saffren again until we know what all this means. Will you do it?"

"That I will!" And she began hastily to get her belongings in marching order. "I'll do anything in the world you'll let me—and oh, I hope they can't do anything to poor, poor Mr. Saffren!"

"Our sporting friend had evidently seen him with Mrs. Harman to-day," I said. "Do you know if they went to the beach again?"

"I only know she meant to meet him—but she

told me she'd be back at the château by four. If I start now——"

"Wasn't the phaeton to be sent to the inn for you?"

"Not until six," she returned briskly, folding her easel and strapping it to her camp-stool with precision. "Isn't it shorter by the woods?"

"You've only to follow this path to the second crossing and then turn to the right," I responded. "I shall hurry back to Madame Brossard's to see Keredec—and here"—I extended my hand toward her traps, of which, in a neatly practical fashion, she had made one close pack—"let me have your things, and I'll take care of them at the inn for you. They're heavy, and it's a long trudge."

"You have your own to carry," she answered, swinging the strap over her shoulder. "It's something of a walk for you, too."

"No, no, let me have them," I protested, for the walk before her *was* long and the things would be heavy indeed before it ended.

"Go your ways," she laughed, and as my hand still remained extended she grasped it with her own and gave it a warm and friendly shake. "Hurry!"

And with an optimism which took my breath, she said, "I know *you* can make it come out all right! Besides, I'll help you!"

With that she turned and started manfully upon her journey. I stared after her for a moment or more, watching the pretty brown dress flashing in and out of shadow among the ragged greeneries, shafts of sunshine now and then flashing upon her hair. Then I picked up my own pack and set out for the inn.

Every one knows that the more serious and urgent the errand a man may be upon, the more incongruous are apt to be the thoughts that skip into his mind. As I went through the woods that day, breathless with haste and curious fears, my brain became suddenly, unaccountably busy with a dream I had had, two nights before. I had not recalled this dream on waking: the recollection of it came to me now for the first time. It was a usual enough dream, wandering and unlifelike, not worth the telling; and I had been thinking so constantly of Mrs. Harman that there was nothing extraordinary in her worthless ex-husband's being part of it.

And yet, looking back upon that last, hurried walk

of mine through the forest, I see how strange it was that I could not quit remembering how in my dream I had gone motoring up Mount Pilatus with the man I had seen so pitiably demolished on the Versailles road, two years before—Larrabee Harman.

CHAPTER XVII

KEREDEC was alone in his salon, extended at ease upon a long chair, an ottoman and a stool, when I burst in upon him; a portentous volume was in his lap, and a prolific pipe, smoking up from his great cloud of beard, gave the final reality to the likeness he thus presented of a range of hills ending in a volcano. But he rolled the book cavalierly to the floor, limbered up by sections to receive me, and offered me a hearty welcome.

"Ha, my dear sir," he cried, "you take pity on the lonely Keredec; you make him a visit. I could not wish better for myself. We shall have a good smoke and a good talk."

"You are improved to-day?" I asked, it may be a little slyly.

"Improve?" he repeated inquiringly.

"Your rheumatism, I mean."

"Ha, yes; that rheumatism!" he shouted, and throwing back his head, rocked the room with sudden laughter. "Hew! But it is gone—almost!

227

Oh, I am much better, and soon I shall be able
to go in the woods again with my boy." He pushed
a chair toward me. "Come, light your cigar; he
will not return for an hour perhaps, and there is
plenty of time for the smoke to blow away. So!
It is better. Now we shall talk."

"Yes," I said, "I wanted to talk with you."

"That is a—what you call?—ha, yes, a coincidence," he returned, stretching himself again in the
long chair, "a happy coincidence; for I have wished
a talk with you; but you are away so early for all
day, and in the evening Oliver, he is always here."

"I think what I wanted to talk about concerns
him particularly."

"Yes?" The professor leaned forward, looking
at me gravely. "That is another coincidence. But
you shall speak first. Commence then."

"I feel that you know me at least well enough,"
I began rather hesitatingly, "to be sure that I
would not, for the world, make any effort to in-
trude in your affairs, or Mr. Saffren's, and that I
would not force your confidence in the remotest——"

"No, no, no!" he interrupted. "Please do not
fear I shall misinterpretate whatever you will say.
You are our friend. We know it."

"Very well," I pursued; "then I speak with no
fear of offending. When you first came to the inn
I couldn't help seeing that you took a great many
precautions for secrecy; and when you afterward
explained these precautions to me on the ground
that you feared somebody might think Mr. Saffren
not quite sane, and that such an impression might
injure him later—well, I could not help seeing
that your explanation did not cover all the ground."

"It is true—it did not." He ran his huge hand
through the heavy white waves of his hair, and
shook his head vigorously. "No; I knew it, my
dear sir, I knew it well. But, what could I do?
I would not have telled my own mother! This
much I can say to you: we came here at a risk,
but I thought that with great care it might be made
little. And I thought a great good thing might be
accomplish if we should come here, something so
fine, so wonderful, that even if the danger had been
great I would have risked it. I will tell you a little
more: I think that great thing is *being* accomplish!"
Here he rose to his feet excitedly and began to pace
the room as he talked, the ancient floor shaking
with his tread. "I think it is *done!* And ha! my
dear sir, if it *should* be, this big Keredec will not

have lived in vain! It was a great task I undertake with my young man, and the glory to see it finish is almost here. Even if the danger should come, the *thing* is done, for all that is real and has true meaning is inside the soul!"

"It was in connection with the risk you have mentioned that I came to talk," I returned with some emphasis, for I was convinced of the reality of Mr. Earl Percy and also very certain that he had no existence inside or outside a soul. "I think it necessary that you should know——"

But the professor was launched. I might as well have swept the rising tide with a broom. He talked with magnificent vehemence for twenty minutes, his theme being some theory of his own that the individuality of a soul is immortal, and that even in perfection, the soul cannot possibly merge into any Nirvana. Meantime, I wondered how Mr. Percy was employing his time, but after one or two ineffectual attempts to interrupt, I gave myself to silence until the oration should be concluded.

"And so it is with my boy," he proclaimed, coming at last to the case in hand. "The spirit of him, the real Oliver Saffren, *that* has *never* change! The outside of him, those thing that *belong* to him,

like his memory, *they* have change, but not himself,
for himself is eternal and unchangeable. I have
taught him, yes; I have helped him get the small
things we can add to our possession—a little knowledge, maybe, a little power of judgment. But, my
dear sir, I tell you that such things are *only* possessions of a man. They are not the *man!* All
that a man *is* or ever shall be, he is when he is a
baby. So with Oliver; he had lived a little while,
twenty-six years, perhaps, when *pft*—like that!—
he became almost as a baby again. He could remember how to talk, but not much more. He
had lost his belongings—they were gone from the
lobe of the brain where he had stored them; but
he was not gone, no part of the real *himself* was
lacking. Then presently they send him to me to
make new his belongings, to restore his possessions.
Ha, what a task! To take him with nothing in the
world of his own and see that he get only *good*
possessions, *good* knowledge, *good* experience! I
took him to the mountains of the Tyrol—two
years—and there his body became strong and splendid while his brain was taking in the stores. It
was quick, for his brain had retained some habits;
it was not a baby's brain, and some small part of

its old stores had not been lost. But if anything useless or bad remain, we empty it out—I and those mountain' with their pure air. Now, I say he is all good and the work was good; I am proud! But I wish to restore *all* that was good in his life; your Keredec is something of a poet.—You may put it: much the old fool! And for that greates' restoration of all I have brought my boy back to France; since it was necessary. It was a madness, and I thank the good God I was mad enough to do it. I cannot tell you yet, my dear sir; but you shall see, you shall see what the folly of that old Keredec has done! You shall see, you shall—and I promise it—what a Paradise, when the good God helps, an old fool's dream can make!"

A half-light had broken upon me as he talked, pacing the floor, thundering his pæan of triumph, his Titanic gestures bruising the harmless air. Only one explanation, incredible, but possible, sufficed. Anything was possible, I thought—anything was probable—with this dreamer whom the trump of Fame, executing a whimsical fantasia, proclaimed a man of science!

"By the wildest chance," I gasped, "you don't mean that you wanted him to fall in love——"

He had reached the other end of the room, but at this he whirled about on me, his laughter rolling out again, till it might have been heard at Père Baudry's.

"Ha, my dear sir, you have said it! But you knew it; you told him to come to me and tell me."

"But I mean that you—unless I utterly mis-understand—you seem to imply that you had selected some one now in France whom you planned that he should care for—that you had selected the lady whom you know as Madame d'Armand."

"Again," he shouted, "you have said it!"

"Professor Keredec," I returned, with asperity, "I have no idea how you came to conceive such a preposterous scheme, but I agree heartily that the word for it is madness. In the first place, I must tell you that her name is not even d'Armand——"

"My dear sir, I know. It was the mistake of that absurd Amédée. She is Mrs. Harman."

"You knew it?" I cried, hopelessly confused. "But Oliver still speaks of her as Madame d'Armand."

"He does not know. She has not told him."

"But why haven't you told him?"

"Ha, that is a story, a poem," he cried, beginning to pace the floor again—"a ballad as old as the oldest of Provence! There is a reason, my dear sir, which I cannot tell you, but it lies within the romance of what you agree is my madness. Some day, I hope, you shall understand and applaud! In the meantime——"

"In the meantime," I said sharply, as he paused for breath, "there is a keen-faced young man who took a room in the inn this morning and who has come to spy upon you, I believe."

"What is it you say?"

He came to a sudden stop.

I had not meant to deliver my information quite so abruptly, but there was no help for it now, and I repeated the statement, giving him a terse account of my two encounters with the rattish youth, and adding:

"He seemed to be certain that 'Oliver Saffren' is an assumed name, and he made a threatening reference to the laws of France."

The effect upon Keredec was a very distinct pallor. He faced me silently until I had finished, then in a voice grown suddenly husky, asked:

"Do you think he came back to the inn? Is
he here now?"

"I do not know."

"We must learn; I must know that, at once."
And he went to the door.

"Let me go instead," I suggested.

"It can't make little difference if he see me,"
said the professor, swallowing with difficulty and
displaying, as he turned to me, a look of such profound anxiety that I was as sorry for him now as
I had been irritated a few minutes earlier by his
galliard air-castles. "I do not know this man,
nor does he know me, but I have fear"—his beard
moved as though his chin were trembling—"I have
fear that I know his employers. Still, it may be
better if you go. Bring somebody here that we
can ask."

"Shall I find Amédée?"

"No, no, no! That babbler? Find Madame
Brossard."

I stepped out to the gallery, to discover Madame
Brossard emerging from a door on the opposite
side of the courtyard; Amédée, Glouglou, and a
couple of carters deploying before her with some
light trunks and bags, which they were carrying

into the passage she had just quitted. I summoned
her quietly; she came briskly up the steps and into
the room, and I closed the door.

"Madame Brossard," said the professor, "you
have a new client to-day."

"That monsieur who arrived this morning," I
suggested.

"He was an American," said the hostess, knitting
her dark brows—"but I do not think that he was
exactly a monsieur."

"Bravo!" I murmured. "That sketches a likeness. It is this 'Percy' without a doubt."

"That is it," she returned. "Monsieur Poissy
is the name he gave."

"Is he at the inn now?"

"No, monsieur, but two friends for whom he
engaged apartments have just arrived."

"Who are they?" asked Keredec quickly.

"It is a lady and a monsieur from Paris. But
not married: they have taken separate apartments
and she has a domestic with her, a negress,
Algerian."

"What are their names?"

"It is not ten minutes that they are installed.
They have not given me their names."

"What is the lady's appearance?"

"Monsieur the Professor," replied the hostess demurely, "she is not beautiful."

"But what is she?" demanded Keredec impatiently; and it could be seen that he was striving to control a rising agitation? "Is she blonde? Is she brunette? Is she young? Is she old? Is she French, English, Spanish——"

"I think," said Madame Brossard, "I think one would call her Spanish, but she is very fat, not young, and with a great deal too much rouge——"

She stopped with an audible intake of breath, staring at my friend's white face. "Eh! it is bad news?" she cried. "And when one has been so ill——"

Keredec checked her with an imperious gesture. "Monsieur Saffren and I leave at once," he said. "I shall meet him on the road; he will not return to the inn. We go to—to Trouville. See that no one knows that we have gone until to-morrow, if possible; I shall leave fees for the servants with you. Go now, prepare your bill, and bring it to me at once. I shall write you where to send our trunks. Quick! And you, my friend"—he turned to me as Madame Brossard, obviously distressed

and frightened, but none the less intelligent for
that, skurried away to do his bidding—"my friend,
will you help us? For we need it!"

"Anything in the world!"

"Go to Père Baudry's; have him put the least
tired of his three horses to his lightest cart and
wait in the road beyond the cottage. Stand in the
road yourself while that is being done. Oliver will
come that way; detain him. I will join you there;
I have only to see to my papers—at the most,
twenty minutes. Go quickly, my friend!"

I strode to the door and out to the gallery. I
was half-way down the steps before I saw that
Oliver Saffren was already in the courtyard, coming
toward me from the archway with a light and
buoyant step.

He looked up, waving his hat to me, his face
lighted with a happiness most remarkable, and
brighter, even, than the strong, midsummer sunshine flaming over him. Dressed in white as he was,
and with the air of victory he wore, he might have
been, at that moment, a figure from some marble
triumph; youthful, conquering—crowned with the
laurel.

I had time only to glance at him, to "take"

him, as it were, between two shutter-flicks of the instantaneous eyelid, and with him, the courtyard flooded with sunshine, the figure of Madame Brossard emerging from her little office, Amédée coming from the kitchen bearing a white-covered tray, and, entering from the road, upon the trail of Saffren but still in the shadow of the archway, the discordant fineries and hatchet-face of the ex-pedestrian and tourist, my antagonist of the forest.

I had opened my mouth to call a warning.

"Hurry" was the word I would have said, but it stopped at "hur—." The second syllable was never uttered.

There came a violent outcry, raucous and shrill as the wail of a captured hen, and out of the passage across the courtyard floundered a woman, fantastically dressed in green and gold.

Her coarse blue-black hair fell dishevelled upon her shoulders, from which her gown hung precariously unfastened, as if she had abandoned her toilet half-way. She was abundantly fat, double-chinned, coarse, greasy, smeared with blue pencillings, carmine, enamel, and rouge.

At the scream Saffren turned. She made straight at him, crying wildly:

"Enfin! Mon mari, mon mari—c'est moi! C'est ta femme, mon cœur!"

She threw herself upon him, her arms about his neck, with a tropical ferocity that was a very paroxysm of triumph.

"Embrasse moi, Larrabi! Embrasse moi!" she cried.

Horrified, outraged, his eyes blazing, he flung her off with a violence surpassing her own, and with loathing unspeakable. She screamed that he was killing her, calling him "husband," and tried to fasten herself upon him again. But he leaped backward beyond the reach of her clutching hands, and, turning, plunged to the steps and staggered up them, the woman following.

From above me leaned the stricken face of Keredec; he caught Saffren under the arm and half lifted him to the gallery, while she strove to hold him by the knees.

"O Christ!" gasped Saffren. "Is *this* the woman?"

The giant swung him across the gallery and into the open door with one great sweep of the arm, strode in after him, and closed and bolted the door. The woman fell in a heap at the foot of the steps, uttered a cracked simulation of the cry of a broken heart.

"Embrasse moi, Larrabi! Embrasse moi!" she cried

"Name of a name of God!" she wailed.   "After all these years!   And my husband strikes me!"

Then it was that what had been in my mind as a monstrous suspicion became a certainty.   For I recognised the woman; she was Mariana—*la bella Mariana la Mursiana.*

If I had ever known Larrabee Harman, if, instead of the two strange glimpses I had caught of him, I had been familiar with his gesture, walk, intonation —even, perhaps, if I had ever heard his voice—the truth might have come to me long ago.

Larrabee Harman!

"Oliver Saffren" was Larrabee Harman.

CHAPTER XVIII

I DO not like to read those poets who write of pain as if they loved it; the study of suffering is for the cold analyst, for the vivisectionist, for those who may transfuse their knowledge of it to the ultimate good of mankind. And although I am so heavily endowed with curiosity concerning the people I find about me, my gift (or curse, whichever it be) knows pause at the gates of the house of calamity. So, if it were possible, I would not speak of the agony of which I was a witness that night in the apartment of my friends at Madame Brossard's. I went with reluctance, but there was no choice. Keredec had sent for me.

. . . When I was about fifteen, a boy cousin of mine, several years younger, terribly injured himself on the Fourth of July; and I sat all night in the room with him, helping his mother. Somehow he had learned that there was no hope of saving his sight; he was an imaginative child and realised the whole meaning of the catastrophe; the eternal darkness. . . . And he understood that the thing had

been done, that there was no going back of it. This
very certainty increased the intensity of his rebellion
a thousandfold. "I *will* have my eyes!" he screamed.
"I *will! I will!*"

Keredec had told his tragic ward too little. The
latter had understood but vaguely the nature of the
catastrophe which overhung his return to France,
and now that it was indeed concrete and definite,
the guardian was forced into fuller disclosures, every
word making the anguish of the listener more intol-
erable. It was the horizonless despair of a child;
and that profound protest I had so often seen
smouldering in his eyes culminated, at its crisis, in
a wild flame of revolt. The shame of the revelation
passed over him; there was nothing of the disastrous drunkard, sober, learning what he had done.
To him, it seemed that he was being forced to suffer
for the sins of another man.

"Do you think that you can make me believe *I*
did this?" he cried. "That I made life unbearable
for *her*, drove *her* from me, and took this hideous,
painted old woman in *her* place? It's a lie. You
can't make me believe such a monstrous lie as that!
You *can't! You can't!*"

He threw himself violently upon the couch, face downward, shuddering from head to foot.

"My poor boy, it is the truth," said Keredec, kneeling beside him and putting a great arm across his shoulders. "It is what a thousand men are doing this night. Nothing is more common, or more unexplainable—or more simple. Of all the nations it is the same, wherever life has become artificial and the poor, foolish young men have too much money and nothing to do. You do not understand it, but our friend here, and I, we understand because we remember what we have been seeing all our life. You say it is not you who did such crazy, horrible things, and you are right. When this poor woman who is so painted and greasy first caught you, when you began to give your money and your time and your life to her, when she got you into this horrible marriage with her, you were blind—you went staggering, in a bad dream; your soul hid away, far down inside you, with its hands over its face. If it could have once stood straight, if the eyes of your body could have once been clean for it to look through, if you could have once been as you are to-day, or as you were when you were a little child, you would have cry out with horror both of her and of yourself,

as you do now; and you would have run away from
her and from everything you had put in your life.
But, in your suffering you must rejoice: the triumph
is that your mind hates that old life as greatly as
your soul hates it. You are as good as if you had
never been the wild fellow—yes, the wicked fellow—
that you were. For a man who shakes off his sin
is clean; he stands as pure as if he had never sinned.
But though his emancipation can be so perfect,
there is a law that he cannot escape from the
result of all the bad and foolish things he has
done, for every act, every breath you draw, is
immortal, and each has a consequence that is
never ending. And so, now, though you are puri-
fied, the suffering from these old actions is here,
and you must abide it. Ah, but that is a little
thing, nothing!—that suffering—compared to what
you have gained, for you have gained your own
soul!"

The desperate young man on the couch answered
only with the sobbing of a broken-hearted child.

I came back to my pavilion after midnight, but
I did not sleep, though I lay upon my bed until
dawn. Then I went for a long, hard walk, break-
fasted at Dives, and begged a ride back to Madame

Brossard's in a peasant's cart which was going that way.

I found George Ward waiting for me on the little veranda of the pavilion, looking handsomer and more prosperously distinguished and distinguishedly prosperous and generally well-conditioned than ever—as I told him.

"I have some news for you," he said after the hearty greeting—"an announcement, in fact."

"Wait!" I glanced at the interested attitude of Mr. Earl Percy, who was breakfasting at a table significantly near the gallery steps, and led the way into the pavilion. "You may as well not tell it in the hearing of that young man," I said, when the door was closed. "He is eccentric."

"So I gathered," returned Ward, smiling, "from his attire. But it really wouldn't matter who heard it. Elizabeth's going to marry Cresson Ingle."

"That is the news—the announcement—you spoke of?"

"Yes, that is it."

To save my life I could not have told at that moment what else I had expected, or feared, that he might say, but certainly I took a deep breath of relief. "I am very glad," I said. "It should be a happy alliance."

"On the whole, I think it will be," he returned thoughtfully. "Ingle's done his share of hard living, and I once had a notion"—he glanced smiling at me—"well, I dare say you know my notion. But it is a good match for Elizabeth and not without advantages on many counts. You see, it's time I married, myself; she feels that very strongly and I think her decision to accept Ingle is partly due to her wish to make all clear for a new mistress of my household,—though that's putting it in a rather grandiloquent way." He laughed. "And as you probably guess, I have an idea that some such arrangement might be somewhere on the wings of the wind on its way to me, before long."

He laughed again, but I did not, and noting my silence he turned upon me a more scrutinising look than he had yet given me, and said:

"My dear fellow, is something the matter? You look quite haggard. You haven't been ill?"

"No, I've had a bad night. That's all."

"Oh, I heard something of a riotous scene taking place over here," he said. "One of the gardeners was talking about it to Elizabeth. Your bad night wouldn't be connected with that, would it? You haven't been playing Samaritan?"

"What was it you heard?" I asked quickly.

"I didn't pay much attention. He said that there was great excitement at Madame Brossard's, because a strange woman had turned up and claimed an insane young man at the inn for her husband, and that they had a fight of some sort——"

"Damnation!" I started from my chair. "Did Mrs. Harman hear this story?"

"Not last night, I'm certain. Elizabeth said the gardener told her as she came down to the château gates to meet me when I arrived—it was late, and Louise had already gone to her room. In fact, I have not seen her yet. But what difference could it possibly make whether she heard it or not? She doesn't know these people, surely?"

"She knows the man."

"This insane——"

"He is not insane," I interrupted. "He has lost the memory of his earlier life—lost it through an accident. You and I saw the accident."

"That's impossible," said George, frowning. "I never saw but one accident that you——"

"That was the one: the man is Larrabee Harman."

George had struck a match to light a cigar; but the operation remained incomplete: he dropped the match upon the floor and set his foot upon it. "Well, tell me about it," he said.

"You haven't heard anything about him since the accident?"

"Only that he did eventually recover and was taken away from the hospital. I heard that his mind was impaired. Does Louise—" he began; stopped, and cleared his throat. "Has Mrs. Harman heard that he is here?"

"Yes; she has seen him."

"Do you mean the scoundrel has been bothering her? Elizabeth didn't tell me of this——"

"Your sister doesn't know," I said, lifting my hand to check him. "I think you ought to understand the whole case—if you'll let me tell you what I know about it."

"Go ahead," he bade me. "I'll try to listen patiently, though the very thought of the fellow has always set my teeth on edge."

"He's not at all what you think," I said. "There's an enormous difference, almost impossible to explain to you, but something you'd understand at once if you saw him. It's such a difference, in fact, that when I found that he was Larrabee Harman the revelation was inexpressibly shocking and distressing to me. He came here under another name; I had no suspicion that he was any one I'd ever heard of, much less that I'd actually seen him twice, two years ago, and I've grown to—well, in truth, to be fond of him."

"What is the change?" asked Ward, and his voice showed that he was greatly disquieted. "What is he like?"

"As well as I can tell you, he's like an odd but very engaging boy, with something pathetic about him; quite splendidly handsome——"

"Oh, he had good looks to spare when I first knew him," George said bitterly. "I dare say he's got them back if he's taken care of himself, or been taken care of, rather! But go on; I won't interrupt you again. Why did he come here? Hoping to see——"

"No. When he came here he did not know of her existence except in the vaguest way. But to go back to that, I'd better tell you first that the woman we saw with him, one day on the boulevard, and who was in the accident with him——"

"La Mursiana, the dancer; I know."

"She had got him to go through a marriage with her——"

"*What?*" Ward's eyes flashed as he shouted the word.

"It seems inexplicable; but as I understand it, he was never quite sober at that time; he had begun to use drugs, and was often in a half-stupefied condition. As a matter of fact, the woman did what she pleased with him. There's no doubt about the validity of the marriage. And what makes it so desperate a muddle is that since the marriage she's taken good care to give no grounds upon which a divorce could be obtained for Harman. She means to hang on."

"I'm glad of that!" said George, striking his knee with his open palm. "That will go a great way toward——"

He paused, and asked suddenly: "Did this marriage take place in France?"

"Yes. You'd better hear me through," I remonstrated. "When he was taken from the hospital, he was placed in charge of a Professor Keredec, a madman of whom you've probably heard."

"Madman? Why, no; he's a member of the

Institute; a psychologist or metaphysician, isn't he?— at any rate of considerable celebrity."

"Nevertheless," I insisted grimly, "as misty a vapourer as I ever saw; a poetic, self-contradicting and inconsistent orator, a blower of bubbles, a seer of visions, a mystic, and a dreamer—about as scientific as Alice's White Knight! Harman's aunt, who lived in London, the only relative he had left, I believe —and she has died since—put him in Keredec's charge, and he was taken up into the Tyrol and virtually hidden for two years, the idea being literally to give him something like an education—Keredec's phrase is 'restore mind to his soul'! What must have been quite as vital was to get him out of his horrible wife's clutches. And they did it, for she could not find him. But she picked up that rat in the garden out yonder—he'd been some sort of stable-manager for Harman once—and set him on the track. He ran the poor boy down, and yesterday she followed him. Now it amounts to a species of sordid siege."

"She wants money, of course."

"Yes, *more* money; a fair allowance has always been sent to her. Keredec has interviewed her notary and she wants a settlement, naming a sum actually larger than the whole estate amounts to. There were colossal expenditures and equally large shrinkages; what he has left is invested in English securities and is not a fortune, but of course she won't believe that and refuses to budge until this impossible settlement is made. You can imagine about how competent such a man as Keredec would be to deal with the situation. In the mean time, his ward is in so dreadful a state of horror and grief I am afraid it is possible that his mind may really give way, for it was not in a normal condition, of course, though he's perfectly sane, as I tell you. If it should," I concluded, with some bitterness, "I suppose Keredec will be still prating upliftingly on the saving of his soul!"

"When was it that Louise saw him?"

"Ah, that," I said, "is where Keredec has been a poet and a dreamer indeed. It was his *plan* that they should meet."

"You mean he brought this wreck of Harman, these husks and shreds of a man, down here for Louise to see?" Ward cried incredulously. "Oh, monstrous!"

"No," I answered. "Only insane. Not because there is anything lacking in Oliver—in Harman,

I mean—for I think that will be righted in time, but because the second marriage makes it a useless cruelty that he should have been allowed to fall in love with his first wife again. Yet that was Keredec's idea of a 'beautiful restoration,' as he calls it!"

"There is something behind all this that you don't know," said Ward slowly. "I'll tell you after I've seen this Keredec. When did the man make you his confidant?"

"Last night. Most of what I learned was as much a revelation to his victim as it was to me. Harman did not know till then that the lady he had been meeting had been his wife, or that he had ever seen her before he came here. He had mistaken her name and she did not enlighten him."

"Meeting?" said Ward harshly. "You speak as if——"

"They have been meeting every day, George."

"I won't believe it of her!" he cried. "She couldn't——"

"It's true. He spoke to her in the woods one day; I was there and saw it. I know now that she knew him at once; and she ran away, but—not in anger. I shouldn't be a very good friend of yours," I went on gently, "if I didn't give you the truth. They've been together every day since then, and I'm afraid—miserably afraid, Ward— that her old feeling for him has been revived."

I have heard Ward use an oath only two or three times in my life, and this was one of them.

"Oh, by God!" he cried, starting to his feet; "I *should* like to meet Professor Keredec!"

"I am at your service, my dear sir," said a deep voice from the veranda. And opening the door, the professor walked into the room.

CHAPTER XIX

HE looked old and tired and sad; it was plain that he expected attack and equally plain that he would meet it with fanatic serenity. And yet, the magnificent blunderer presented so fine an aspect of the tortured Olympian, he confronted us with so vast a dignity—the driven snow of his hair tousled upon his head and shoulders, like a storm in the higher altitudes—that he regained, in my eyes, something of his mountain grandeur before he had spoken a word in defence. But sympathy is not what one should be entertaining for an antagonist; therefore I said cavalierly:

"This is Mr. Ward, Professor Keredec. He is Mrs. Harman's cousin and close friend."

"I had divined it." The professor made a French bow, and George responded with as slight a salutation as it has been my lot to see.

"We were speaking of your reasons," I continued, "for bringing Mr. Harman to this place. Frankly, we were questioning your motive."

"My motives? I have wished to restore to two young people the paradise which they had lost".

Ward uttered an exclamation none the less violent because it was half-suppressed, while, for my part, I laughed outright; and as Keredec turned his eyes questioningly upon me, I said:

"Professor Keredec, you'd better understand at once that I mean to help undo the harm you've done. I couldn't tell you last night, in Harman's presence, but I think you're responsible for the whole ghastly tragi-comedy—as hopeless a tangle as ever was made on this earth!"

This was even more roughly spoken than I had intended, but it did not cause him to look less mildly upon me, nor was there the faintest shadow of resentment in his big voice when he replied:

"In this world things may be tangled, they may be sad, yet they may be good."

"I'm afraid that seems rather a trite generality. I beg you to remember that plain-speaking is of some importance just now."

"I shall remember."

"Then we should be glad of the explanation," said Ward, resting his arms on my table and leaning across it toward Keredec.

"We should, indeed," I echoed.

"It is simple," began the professor. "I learned my poor boy's history well, from those who could tell me, from his papers—yes, and from the bundles of old-time letters which were given me—since it was necessary that I should know everything. From all these I learned what a strong and beautiful soul was that lady who loved him so much that she ran away from her home for his sake. *Hélas!* he was already the slave of what was bad and foolish, he had gone too far from himself, was overlaid with the habit of evil, and she could not save him then. The spirit was dying in him, although it was there, and *it* was good——"

Ward's acrid laughter rang out in the room, and my admiration went unwillingly to Keredec for the way he took it, which was to bow gravely, as if acknowledging the other's right to his own point of view.

"If you will study the antique busts," he said, "you will find that Socrates is Silenus dignified. I choose to believe in the infinite capacities of all men—and in the spirit in all. And so I try to restore my poor boy his capacities and his spirit. But that was not all. The time was coming when I could do

no more for him, when the little education of books
would be finish' and he must go out in the world
again to learn—all newly—how to make of himself
a man of use. That is the time of danger, and the
thought was troubling me when I learned that
Madame Harman was here, near this inn, of which
I knew. So I brought him."

"The inconceivable selfishness, the devilish brutality of it!" Ward's face was scarlet. "You
didn't care how you sacrificed her——"

"Sacrificed!" The professor suddenly released
the huge volume of his voice. "Sacrificed!" he
thundered. "If I could give him back to her as
he is now, it would be restoring to her all that she
had loved in him, the real *self* of him! It would
be the greatest gift in her life."

"You speak for her?" demanded Ward, the question coming like a lawyer's. It failed to disturb
Keredec, who replied quietly:

"It is a quibble. I speak for her, yes, my dear
sir. Her action in defiance of her family and her
friends proved the strength of what she felt for the
man she married; that she have remained with him
three years—until it was impossible—proved its
persistence; her letters, which I read with reverence,

proved its beauty—to me. It was a living passion, one that could not die. To let them see each other again; that was all I intended. To give them their new chance—and then, for myself, to keep out of the way. That was why—" he turned to me—"that was why I have been guilty of pretending to have that bad rheumatism, and I hope you will not think it an ugly trick of me! It was to give him his chance freely; and though at first I had much anxiety it was done. In spite of all his wicked follies theirs had been a true love, and nothing in this world could be more inevitable than that they should come together again if the chance could be given. And they *have*, my dear sirs! It has so happened. To him it has been a wooing as if for the first time; so she has preferred it, keeping him to his mistake of her name. She feared that if he knew that it was the same as his own he might ask questions of me, and, you see, she did not know that I had made this little plan, and was afraid——"

"We are not questioning Mrs. Harman's motives," George interrupted hotly, "but *yours!*"

"Very well, my dear sir; that is all. I have explained them."

"You have?" I interjected. "Then, my dear Keredec, either you are really insane or I am! You knew that this poor, unfortunate devil of a Harman was tied to that hyenic prowler yonder who means to fatten on him, and will never release him; you knew that. Then why did you bring him down here to fall in love with a woman he he can never have? In pity's name, if you didn't hope to half kill them both, what *did* you mean?"

"My dear fellow," interposed George quickly, "you underrate Professor Keredec's shrewdness. His plans are not so simple as you think. He knows that my cousin Louise never obtained a divorce from her husband."

"What?" I said, not immediately comprehending his meaning.

"I say, Mrs. Harman never obtained a divorce."

"Are you delirious?" I gasped.

"It's the truth; she never did."

"I saw a notice of it at the time. 'A notice?' I saw a hundred!"

"No. What you saw was that she had made an application for divorce. Her family got her that far and then she revolted. The suit was dropped."

"It is true, indeed," said Keredec. "The poor boy was on the other side of the world, and he thought it was granted. He had been bad before, but from that time he cared nothing what became of him. That was the reason this Spanish woman——"

I turned upon him sharply. "*You* knew it?"

"It is a year that I have known it; when his estate was—"

"Then why didn't you tell me last night?"

"My dear sir, I could not in *his* presence, because it is one thing I dare not let him know. This Spanish woman is so hideous, her claim upon him is so horrible to him I could not hope to control him—he would shout it out to her that she cannot call him husband. God knows what he would do!"

"Well, why shouldn't he shout it out to her?"

"You do not understand," George interposed again, "that what Professor Keredec risked for his 'poor boy,' in returning to France, was a trial on the charge of bigamy!"

The professor recoiled from the definite brutality. "My dear sir! It is not possible that such a thing can happen."

"I conceive it very likely to happen," said George,

"unless you get him out of the country before the lady now installed here as his wife discovers the truth."

"But she must not!" Keredec lifted both hands toward Ward appealingly; they trembled, and his voice betrayed profound agitation. "She cannot! She has never suspected such a thing; there is nothing that could *make* her suspect it!"

"One particular thing would be my telling her," said Ward quietly.

"Never!" cried the professor, stepping back from him. "You could not do that!"

"I not only could, but I will, unless you get him out of the country—and quickly!"

"George!" I exclaimed, coming forward between them. "This won't do at all. You can't——"

"That's enough," he said, waving me back, and I saw that his hand was shaking, too, like Keredec's. His face had grown very white; but he controlled himself to speak with a coolness that made what he said painfully convincing. "I know what you think," he went on, addressing me, "but you're wrong. It isn't for myself. When I sailed for New York in the spring I thought there was a chance that she would carry out the action she begun four years ago and go through the form of ridding herself of him definitely; that is, I thought there was some hope for me; I believed there was until this morning. But I know better now. If she's seen him again, and he's been anything except literally unbearable, it's all over with *me*. From the first, I never had a chance against him; he was a hard rival, even when he'd become only a cruel memory." His voice rose. "I've lived a sober, decent life, and I've treated *her* with gentleness and reverence since she was born, and *he's* done nothing but make a stewpan of his life and neglect and betray her when he had her. Heaven knows why it is; it isn't because of anything he's done or has, it's just because it's *him*, I suppose, but I know my chance is gone for good! *That* leaves me free to act for her; no one can accuse me of doing it for myself. And I swear she sha'n't go through that slough of despond again while I have breath in my body!"

"Steady, George!" I said.

"Oh, I'm steady enough," he cried. "Professor Keredec shall be convinced of it! My cousin is not going into the mire again; she shall be freed of it for ever: I speak as her relative now, the representative of her family and of those who care for her happiness and good. Now she *shall* make the separation definite—and *legal!* And let Professor Keredec get his 'poor boy' out of the country. Let him do it quickly! I make it as a condition of my not informing the woman yonder and her lawyer. And by my hope of salvation I warn you——"

"George, for pity's sake!" I shouted, throwing my arm about his shoulders, for his voice had risen to a pitch of excitement and fury that I feared must bring the whole place upon us. He caught himself up suddenly, stared at me blankly for a moment, then sank into a chair with a groan. As he did so, I became aware of a sound that had been worrying my subconsciousness for an indefinite length of time, and realised what it was. Some one was knocking for admission.

I crossed the room and opened the door. Miss Elizabeth stood there, red-faced and flustered, and behind her stood Mr. Cresson Ingle, who looked dubiously amused.

"Ah—come in," I said awkwardly. "George is here. Let me present Professor Keredec——"

" 'George is here!' " echoed Miss Elizabeth, interrupting, and paying no attention whatever to an agitated bow on the part of the professor. "I should say he *was!* They probably know *that* all the way to Trouville!"

"We were discussing——" I began.

"Ah, I know what you were discussing," she said impatiently. "Come in, Cresson." She turned to Mr. Ingle, who was obviously reluctant. "It is a family matter, and you'll have to go through with it now."

"That reminds me," I said. "May I offer——"

"Not now!" Miss Elizabeth cut short a rather embarrassed handshake which her betrothed and I were exchanging. "I'm in a very nervous and distressed state of mind, as I suppose we all are, for that matter. This morning I learned the true situation over here; and I'm afraid Louise has heard; at least she's not at Quesnay. I got into a panic for fear she had come here, but thank heaven she does not seem to—Good gracious! What's *that?*"

It was the discordant voice of Mariana la Mursiana, crackling in strident protest. My door was still open; I turned to look and saw her, hot-faced, tousle-haired, insufficiently wrapped, striving to ascend the gallery steps, but valiantly opposed by Madame Brossard, who stood in the way.

"But *no*, madame," insisted Madame Brossard, excited but darkly determined. "You cannot ascend. There is nothing on the upper floor of this wing except the apartment of Professor Keredec."

"Name of a dog!" shrilled the other. "It is my husband's apartment, I tell you. *Il y a une femme avec lui!*"

"It is Madame Harman who is there," said Keredec hoarsely in my ear. "I came away and left them together."

"Come," I said, and, letting the others think what they would, sprang across the veranda, the professor beside me, and ran toward the two women who were beginning to struggle with more than their tongues. I leaped by them and up the steps, but Keredec thrust himself between our hostess and her opponent, planting his great bulk on the lowest step. Glancing hurriedly over my shoulder, I saw the Spanish woman strike him furiously upon the breast with both hands, but I knew she would never pass him.

I entered the salon of the "Grande Suite," and closed the door quickly behind me.

Louise Harman was standing at the other end of the room; she wore the pretty dress of white and lilac and the white hat. She looked cool and beautiful and good, and there were tears in her eyes. To come into this quiet chamber and see her so, after the hot sunshine and tawdry scene below, was like leaving the shouting market-place for a shadowy chapel.

Her husband was kneeling beside her; he held one of her hands in both his, her other rested upon his head; and something in their attitudes made me know I had come in upon their leave-taking. But from the face he lifted toward her all trace of his tragedy had passed: the wonder and worship written there left no room for anything else.

"Mrs. Harman—" I began.

"Yes?" she said. "I am coming."

"But I don't want you to. I've come for fear you would, and you—you must not," I stammered. "You must wait."

"Why?"

"It's necessary," I floundered. "There is a scene——"

"I know," she said quietly. "*That* must be, of course."

Harman rose, and she took both his hands, holding them against her breast.

"My dear," she said gently,—"my dearest, you must stay. Will you promise not to pass that door, even, until you have word from me again?"

"Yes," he answered huskily, "if you'll promise it *shall* come—some day?"

"It shall, indeed. Be sure of it."

I had turned away, but I heard the ghost of his voice whispering "good-bye." Then she was beside me and opening the door.

I tried to stay her.

"Mrs. Harman," I urged, "I earnestly beg you——"

"No," she answered, "this is better."

She stepped out upon the gallery; I followed, and she closed the door. Upon the veranda of my pavilion were my visitors from Quesnay, staring up at us apprehensively; Madame Brossard and Keredec still held the foot of the steps, but la Mursiana had abandoned the siege, and, accompanied by Mr. Percy and Rameau, the black-bearded notary, who had joined her, was crossing the garden toward her own apartment.

At the sound of the closing door, she glanced over her shoulder, sent forth a scream, and, whirling about, ran viciously for the steps, where she was again blocked by the indomitable Keredec.

"Ah, you foolish woman, I know who you are," she cried, stepping back from him to shake a menacing hand at the quiet lady by my side. "You want to get yourself into trouble! That man in the room up there has been my husband these two years and more."

"No, madame," said Louise Harman, "you are mistaken; he is my husband."

"But you divorced him," vociferated the other wildly. "You divorced him in America!"

"No. You are mistaken," the quiet voice replied. "The suit was withdrawn. He is still my husband."

I heard the professor's groan of despair, but it was drowned in the wild shriek of Mariana. *"What?* You tell *me* that? Ah, the miserable! If what you say is true, he shall pay bitterly! He shall wish that he had died by fire! What! You think he can marry *me*, break my leg so that I cannot dance again, ruin my career, and then go away with a pretty woman like you and be happy? Aha, there are prisons in France for people who marry two like that; I do not know what they do in *your*

barbaric country, but they are decent people over
here and they punish. He shall pay for it in suffering—" her voice rose to an incredible and unbearable shriek—"and you, *you* shall pay, too! You
can't come stealing honest women's husbands like
that. You shall *pay!*"

I saw George Ward come running forward with
his hand upraised in a gesture of passionate warning, for Mrs. Harman, unnoticed by me—I was
watching the Spanish woman—had descended the
steps and had passed Keredec, walking straight to
Mariana. I leaped down after her, my heart in my
throat, fearing a thousand things.

"You must not talk like that," she said, not lifting her voice—yet every one in the courtyard heard
her distinctly. "You can do neither of us any harm
in the world."

CHAPTER XX

IT is impossible to say what Mariana would have done had there been no interference, for she had worked herself into one of those furies which women of her type can attain when they feel the occasion demands it, a paroxysm none the less dangerous because its foundation is histrionic. But Rameau threw his arms about her; Mr. Percy came hastily to his assistance, and Ward and I sprang in between her and the too-fearless lady she strove to reach. Even at that, the finger-nails of Mariana's right hand touched the pretty white hat—but only touched it and no more.

Rameau and the little spy managed to get their vociferating burden across the courtyard and into her own door, where she suddenly subsided, disappearing within the passage to her apartment in unexpected silence—indubitably a disappointment to the interested Amédée, to Glouglou, François, and the whole personnel of the inn, who hastened to group themselves about the door in attentive attitudes.

"In heaven's name," gasped Miss Elizabeth, seizing her cousin by the arm, "come into the pavilion. Here's the whole world looking at us!"

"Professor Keredec—" Mrs. Harman began, resisting, and turning to the professor appealingly.

"Oh, let him come too!" said Miss Elizabeth desperately. "Nothing could be worse than this!"

She led the way back to the pavilion, and, refusing to consider a proposal on the part of Mr. Ingle and myself to remain outside, entered the room last, herself, producing an effect of "shooing" the rest of us in; closed the door with surprising force, relapsed in a chair, and burst into tears.

"Not a soul at Quesnay," sobbed the mortified chatelaine—"not one but will know this before dinner! They'll hear the whole thing within two hours."

"Isn't there any way of stopping that, at least?" Ward said to me.

"None on earth, unless you go home at once and turn your visitors and *their* servants out of the house," I answered.

"There is nothing they shouldn't know," said Mrs. Harman.

George turned to her with a smile so bravely managed that I was proud of him. "Oh, yes, there is," he said. "We're going to get you out of all this."

"All this?" she repeated.

"All this *mire!*" he answered. "We're going to get you out of it and keep you out of it, now, for good. I don't know whether your revelation to the Spanish woman will make that easier or harder, but I do know that it makes the mire deeper."

"For whom?"

"For Harman. But you sha'n't share it!"

Her anxious eyes grew wider. "How have I made it deeper for him? Wasn't it necessary that the poor woman should be told the truth?"

"Professor Keredec seemed to think it important that she shouldn't."

She turned to Keredec with a frightened gesture and an unintelligible word of appeal, as if entreating him to deny what George had said. The professor's beard was trembling; he looked haggard; an almost pitiable apprehension hung upon his eyelids; but he came forward manfully.

"Madame," he said, "you could never in your life do anything that would make harm. You were right to speak, and I had short sight to fear, since it was the truth."

"But why did you fear it?"

"It was because—" he began, and hesitated.

"I must know the reason," she urged. "I must know just what I've done."

"It was because," he repeated, running a nervous hand through his beard, "because the knowledge would put us so utterly in this people's power. Already they demand more than we could give them; now they can—"

"They can do what?" she asked tremulously.

His eyes rested gently on her blanched and stricken face. "Nothing, my dear lady," he answered, swallowing painfully. "Nothing that will last. I am an old man. I have seen and I have—I have thought. And I tell you that only the real survives; evil actions are some phantoms that disappear. They must not trouble us."

"That is a high plane," George intervened, and he spoke without sarcasm. "To put it roughly, these people have been asking more than the Harman estate is worth; that was on the strength of the woman's claim as a wife; but now they know she is not one, her position is immensely strengthened, for she has only to go before the nearest *Commissaire de Police*——"

"Oh, no!" Mrs. Harman cried passionately. "I haven't done *that!* You mustn't tell me I have. You *mustn't!*"

"Never!" he answered. "There could not be a greater lie than to say you have done it. The responsibility is with the wretched and vicious boy who brought the catastrophe upon himself. But don't you see that you've got to keep out of it, that we've got to take you out of it?"

"You can't! I'm part of it; better or worse, it's as much mine as his."

"No, no!" cried Miss Elizabeth. "*You* mustn't tell us *that!*" Still weeping, she sprang up and threw her arms about her brother. "It's too horrible of you——"

"It is what I must tell you," Mrs. Harman said. "My separation from my husband is over. I shall be with him now for——"

"I won't listen to you!" Miss Elizabeth lifted her wet face from George's shoulder, and there was a note of deep anger in her voice. "You don't know what you're talking about; you haven't the faintest idea of what a hideous situation that creature has made for himself. Don't you know that that awful woman was right, and there are laws in

France? When she finds she can't get out of him all she wants, do you think she's going to let him off? I suppose she struck you as being quite the sort who'd prove nobly magnanimous! Are you so blind you don't see exactly what's going to happen? She'll ask twice as much now as she did before; and the moment it's clear that she isn't going to get it, she'll call in an agent of police. She'll get her money in a separate suit and send him to prison to do it. The case against him is positive; there isn't a shadow of hope for him. You talk of being with him; don't you see how preposterous that is? Do you imagine they encourage family housekeeping in French prisons?"

"Oh, come, this won't do!" The speaker was Cresson Ingle, who stepped forward, to my surprise; for he had been hovering in the background wearing an expression of thorough discomfort.

"You're going much too far," he said, touching his betrothed upon the arm. "My dear Elizabeth, there is no use exaggerating; the case is unpleasant enough just as it is."

"In what have I exaggerated?" she demanded.

"Why, I *knew* Larrabee Harman," he returned. "I knew him fairly well. I went as far as Honolulu

with him, when he and some of his heelers started
round the world; and I remember that papers were
served on him in San Francisco. Mrs. Harman
had made her application; it was just before he
sailed. About a year and a half or two years later
I met him again, in Paris. He was in pretty bad
shape; seemed hypnotised by this Mariana and
afraid as death of her; she could go into a tantrum
that would frighten him into anything. It was
a joke—down along the line of the all-night dancers
and cafés—that she was going to marry him; and
some one told me afterward that she claimed to
have brought it about. I suppose it's true; but
there is no question of his having married her in
good faith. He believed that the divorce had
been granted; he'd offered no opposition to it whatever. He was travelling continually, and I don't
think he knew much of what was going on, even
right around him, most of the time. He began
with cognac and absinthe in the morning, you know.
For myself, I always supposed the suit had been
carried through; so did people generally, I think.
He'll probably have to stand trial, and of course
he's technically guilty, but I don't believe he'd
be convicted—though I must say it would have

been a most devilish good thing for him if he could
have been got out of France before la Mursiana
heard the truth.   Then he could have made terms
with her safely at a distance—she'd have been
powerless to injure him and would have precious
soon come to time and been glad to take whatever
he'd give her.   *Now*, I suppose, that's impossible,
and they'll arrest him if he tries to budge.   But
this talk of prison and all that is nonsense, my
dear Elizabeth!"

"You admit there is a chance of it!" she retorted.

"I've said all I had to say," returned Mr. Ingle
with a dubious laugh.   "And if you don't mind, I
believe I'll wait for you outside, in the machine.
I want to look at the gear-box."

He paused, as if in deference to possible opposition, and, none being manifested, went hastily from
the room with a sigh of relief, giving me, as he
carefully closed the door, a glance of profound
commiseration over his shoulder.

Miss Elizabeth had taken her brother's hand, not
with the effect of clinging for sympathy; nor had
her throwing her arms about him produced that
effect; one could as easily have imagined Brunhilda

hiding her face in a man's coat-lapels. George's
sister wept, not weakly: she was on the defensive,
but not for herself.

"Does the fact that he may possibly escape going
to prison"—she addressed her cousin—"make his
position less scandalous, or can it make the man
himself less detestable?"

Mrs. Harman looked at her steadily. There was
a long and sorrowful pause.

"Nothing is changed," she said finally; her eyes
still fixed gravely on Miss Elizabeth's.

At that, the other's face flamed up, and she
uttered a half-choked exclamation. "Oh," she
cried—"you've fallen in love with playing the
martyr; it's *self*-love! You *see* yourself in the rôle!
No one on earth could make me believe you're in
love with this degraded imbecile—all that's left of
the wreck of a vicious life! It isn't that! It's because you want to make a shining example of
yourself; you want to get down on your knees and
wash off the vileness from this befouled creature;
you want——"

"Madame!" Keredec interrupted tremendously,
"you speak out of no knowledge!" He leaned toward
her across the table, which shook under the weight

of his arms. "There is no vileness; no one who is clean remains befouled because of the things that are gone."

"They do not?" She laughed hysterically, and for my part, I sighed in despair—for there was no stopping him.

"They do not, indeed! Do you know the relation of *time* to this little life of ours? We have only the present moment; your consciousness of that is your existence. Your knowledge of each present moment as it passes—and it passes so swiftly that each word I speak now overlaps it— yet it is all we have. For all the rest, for what has gone by and what is yet coming—*that* has no real existence; it is all a dream. It is not *alive*. It *is* not! It *is*—nothing! So the soul that stands clean and pure to-day *is* clean and pure—and that is all there is to say about that soul!"

"But a soul with evil tendencies," Ward began impatiently, "if one must meet you on your own ground——"

"Ha! my dear sir, those evil tendencies would be in the soiling memories, and my boy is free from them."

"He went toward all that was soiling before.

Surely you can't pretend he may not take that direction again?"

"That," returned the professor quickly, "is his to choose. If this lady can be with him now, he will choose right."

"So!" cried Miss Elizabeth, "you oner her the rôle of a guide, do you? First she is to be his companion through a trial for bigamy in a French court, and, if he is acquitted, his nurse, teacher, and moral preceptor?" She turned swiftly to her cousin. "That's *your* conception of a woman's mission?"

"I haven't any mission," Mrs. Harman answered quietly. "I've never thought about missions; I only know I belong to him; that's all I *ever* thought about it. I don't pretend to explain it, or make it seem reasonable. And when I met him again, here, it was—it was—it was proved to me."

"Proved?" echoed Miss Elizabeth incredulously.

"Yes; proved as certainly as the sun shining proves that it's day."

"Will you tell us?"

It was I who asked the question: I spoke involuntarily, but she did not seem to think it strange that I should ask.

"Oh, when I first met him," she said tremulously, "I was frightened; but it was not he who frightened me—it was the rush of my own feeling. I did not know what I felt, but I thought I might die, and he was so like himself as I had first known him—but so changed, too; there was something so wonderful about him, something that must make any stranger feel sorry for him, and yet it is beautiful—" She stopped for a moment and wiped her eyes, then went on bravely: "And the next day he came, and waited for me—I should have come here for him if he hadn't—and I fell in with the mistake he had made about my name. You see, he'd heard I was called 'Madame d'Armand,' and I wanted him to keep on thinking that, for I thought if he knew I was Mrs. Harman he might find out—" She paused, her lip beginning to tremble. "Oh, don't you see why I didn't want him to know? I didn't want him to suffer as he would—as he does now, poor child!—but most of all I wanted— I wanted to see if he would fall in love with me again! I kept him from knowing, because, if he thought I was a stranger, and the same thing happened again—his caring for me, I mean—" She had begun to weep now, freely and openly, but

not from grief. "Oh!" she cried, "don't you *see*
how it's all proven to me?"

"I see how it has deluded you!" said Miss Elizabeth vehemently. "I see what a rose-light it has
thrown about this creature; but it won't last, thank
God! any more than it did the other time. The
thing is for you to come to your senses before——"

"Ah, my dear, I have come to them at last and
for ever!" The words rang full and strong, though
she was white and shaking, and heavy tears filled
her eyes. "I know what I am doing now, if I never
knew before!"

"You never did know——" Miss Ward began, but
George stopped her.

"Elizabeth!" he said quickly. "We mustn't go on
like this; it's more than any of us can bear. Come,
let's get out into the air; let's get back to Quesnay.
We'll have Ingle drive us around the longer way,
by the sea." He turned to his cousin. "Louise, you'll
come now? If not, we'll have to stay here with you."

"I'll come," she answered, trying bravely to stop
the tears that kept rising in spite of her; "if you'll
wait till"—and suddenly she flashed through them
a smile so charming that my heart ached the harder
for George—"till I can stop crying!"

CHAPTER XXI

MR. EARL PERCY and I sat opposite each other at dinner that evening. Perhaps, for charity's sake, I should add that though we faced each other, and, indeed, eyed each other solemnly at intervals, we partook not of the same repast, having each his own table; his being set in the garden at his constant station near the gallery steps, and mine, some fifty feet distant, upon my own veranda, but moved out from behind the honeysuckle screen, for I sat alone and the night was warm.

To analyse my impression of Mr. Percy's glances, I cannot conscientiously record that I found favour in his eyes. For one thing, I fear he may not have recalled to his bosom a clarion sentiment (which doubtless he had ofttimes cheered from his native gallery in softer years): the honourable declaration that many an honest heart beats beneath a poor man's coat. As for his own attire, he was even as the lilies of Quesnay; that is to say, I beheld upon him the same formation of tie that I had seen there,

the same sensuous beauty of the state waistcoat,
though I think that his buttons were, if anything,
somewhat spicier than those which had awed me at
the château. And when we simultaneously reached
the fragrant hour of coffee, the cigarette case that
glittered in his hand was one for which some lady-
friend of his (I knew intuitively) must have given
her All—and then been left in debt.

Amédée had served us both; Glouglou, as aforetime, attending the silent "Grande Suite," where
the curtains were once more tightly drawn.   Monsieur Rameau dined with his client in her own salon,
evidently; at least, Victorine, the *femme de chambre*,
passed to and from the kitchen in that direction,
bearing laden trays.   When Mr. Percy's cigarette
had been lighted, hesitation marked the manner of
our *maître d'hôtel;* plainly he wavered, but finally
old custom prevailed; abandoning the cigarette, he
chose the cigar, and, hastily clearing my fashionable
opponent's table, approached the pavilion with his
most conversational face.

I greeted him indifferently, but with hidden
pleasure, for my soul (if Keredec is right and I have
one) lay sorrowing.   I needed relief, and whatever
else Amédée was, he was always that.   I spoke first:

"Amédée, how long a walk is it from Quesnay to Père Baudry's?"

"Monsieur, about three-quarters of an hour for a good walker, one might say."

"A long way for Jean Ferret to go for a cup of cider," I remarked musingly.

"Eh? But why should he?" asked Amédée blankly.

"Why indeed? Surely even a Norman gardener lives for more than cider! You usually meet him there about noon, I believe?"

Methought he had the grace to blush, though there is an everlasting doubt in my mind that it may have been the colour of the candle-shade producing that illusion. It was a strange thing to see, at all events, and, taking it for a physiological fact at the time, I let my willing eyes linger upon it as long as it (or its appearance) was upon him.

"You were a little earlier than usual to-day," I continued finally, full of the marvel.

"Monsieur?" He was wholly blank again.

"Weren't you there about eleven? Didn't you go about two hours after Mr. Ward and his friends left here?"

He scratched his head. "I believe I had an

errand in that direction. Eh? Yes, I remember.
Truly, I think it so happened."

"And you found Jean Ferret there?"

"Where, monsieur?"

"At Père Baudry's."

"No, monsieur."

"What?" I exclaimed.

"No, monsieur." He was firm, somewhat re-
proachful.

"You didn't see Jean Ferret this morning?"

"Monsieur?"

"Amédée!"

"Eh, but I did not find him at Père Baudry's!
It may have happened that I stopped there, but he
did not come until some time after."

"After you had gone away from Père Baudry's,
you mean?"

"No, monsieur; after I arrived there. Truly."

"Now we have it! And you gave him the news
of all that had happened here?"

"Monsieur!"

A world—no, a constellation, a universe!—of
reproach was in the word.

"I retract the accusation," I said promptly. "I
meant something else."

"Upon everything that takes place at our hotel here, I am silent to all the world."

"As the grave!" I said with enthusiasm. "Truly —that is a thing well known. But Jean Ferret, then? He is not so discreet; I have suspected that you are in his confidence. At times you have even hinted as much. Can you tell me if he saw the automobile of Monsieur Ingle when it came back to the château after leaving here?"

"It had arrived the moment before he departed."

"Quite *so!* I understand," said I.

"He related to me that Mademoiselle Ward had the appearance of agitation, and Madame d'Armand that of pallor, which was also the case with Monsieur Ward."

"Therefore," I said, "Jean Ferret ran all the way to Père Baudry's to learn from you the reason for this agitation and this pallor?"

"But, monsieur——"

"I retract again!" I cut him off—to save time. "What other news had he?"

There came a gleam into his small, infolded eyes, a tiny glitter reflecting the mellow candle-light, but changing it, in that reflection, to a cold and sinister point of steel. It should have warned me, but, as he paused, I repeated my question.

"Monsieur, people say everything," he answered, frowning as if deploring what they said in some secret, particular instance. "The world is full of idle gossipers, tale-bearers, spreaders of scandal! And, though I speak with perfect respect, all the people at the château are not perfect in such ways."

"Do you mean the domestics?"

"The visitors!"

"What do they say?"

"Eh, well, then, they say—but no!" He contrived a masterly pretense of pained reluctance. "I cannot——"

"Speak out," I commanded, piqued by his shilly-shallying. "What do they say?"

"Monsieur, it is about"—he shifted his weight from one leg to the other—"it is about—about that beautiful Mademoiselle Elliott who sometimes comes here."

This was so far from what I had expected that I was surprised into a slight change of attitude, which all too plainly gratified him, though he made an effort to conceal it. "Well," I said uneasily, "what do they find to say of Mademoiselle Elliott?"

"They say that her painting is only a ruse to see monsieur."

"To see Monsieur Saffren, yes."

"But, no!" he cried. "That is not——"

"Yes, it is," I assured him calmly. "As you know, Monsieur Saffren is very, very handsome, and Mademoiselle Elliott, being a painter, is naturally anxious to look at him from time to time."

"You are sure?" he said wistfully, even plaintively. "That is not the meaning Jean Ferret put upon it."

"He was mistaken."

"It may be, it may be," he returned, greatly crestfallen, picking up his tray and preparing to go. "But Jean Ferret was very positive."

"And I am even more so!"

"Then that malicious maid of Mademoiselle Ward's was mistaken also," he sighed, "when she said that now a marriage is to take place between Mademoiselle Ward and Monsieur Ingle——"

"Proceed," I bade him.

He moved a few feet nearer the kitchen. "The malicious woman said to Jean Ferret——" He paused and coughed. "It was in reference to those Italian jewels monsieur used to send——"

"What about them?" I asked ominously.

"The woman says that Mademoiselle Ward—" he increased the distance between us—"that now she should give them to Mademoiselle Elliott! *Good* night, monsieur!"

His entrance into the kitchen was precipitate. I sank down again into the wicker chair (from which I had hastily risen) and contemplated the stars. But the short reverie into which I then fell was interrupted by Mr. Percy, who, sauntering leisurely about the garden, paused to address me.

"You folks thinks you was all to the gud, gittin' them trunks off, what?"

"You speak in mysterious numbers," I returned, having no comprehension of his meaning.

"I suppose you don' know nothin' about it," he laughed satirically. "You didn' go over to Lisieux 'saft'noon to ship 'em? Oh, no, not *you!*"

"I went for a long walk this afternoon, Mr. Percy. Naturally, I couldn't have walked so far as Lisieux and back."

"Luk here, m'friend," he said sharply—"I reco'-nise 'at you're tryin' t' play your own hand, but I ast you as man to man: *Do* you think you got any chanst t' git that feller off t' Paris?"

"*Do* you think it will rain to-night?" I inquired.

The light of a reflecting lamp which hung on the wall near the archway enabled me to perceive a bitter frown upon his forehead. "When a gen'leman asts a question *as* a gen'leman," he said, his voice expressing a noble pathos, "I can't see no call for no other gen'leman to go an' play the smart Aleck and not answer him."

In simple dignity he turned his back upon me and strolled to the other end of the courtyard, leaving me to the renewal of my reverie.

It was not a happy one.

My friends—old and new—I saw inextricably caught in a tangle of cross-purposes, miserably and hopelessly involved in a situation for which I could predict no possible relief. I was able to understand now the beauty as well as the madness of Keredec's plan; and I had told him so (after the departure of the Quesnay party), asking his pardon for my brusquerie of the morning. But the towering edifice his hopes had erected was now tumbled about his ears: he had failed to elude the Mursiana. There could be no doubt of her absolute control of the situation. *That* was evident in the every step of the youth now confidently parading before me.

Following his active stride with my eye, I observed him in the act of saluting, with a gracious nod of his bare head, some one, invisible to me, who was approaching from the road. Immediately after—and altogether with the air of a person merely "happening in"—a slight figure, clad in a long coat, a short skirt, and a broad-brimmed, veil-bound brown hat, sauntered casually through the archway and came into full view in the light of the reflector.

I sprang to my feet and started toward her, uttering an exclamation which I was unable to stifle, though I tried to.

"Good evening, Mr. Percy," she said cheerily. "It's the most *exuberant* night. *You're* quite hearty, I hope?"

"Takin' a walk, I see, little lady," he observed with genial patronage.

"Oh, not just for that," she returned. "It's more to see *him*." She nodded to me, and, as I reached her, carelessly gave me her left hand. "You know I'm studying with him," she continued to Mr. Percy, exhibiting a sketch-book under her arm. "I dropped over to get a criticism."

"Oh, drawin'-lessons?" said Mr. Precy tolerantly. "Well, don' lemme interrup' ye."

He moved as if to withdraw toward the steps, but she detained him with a question. "You're spending the rest of the summer here?"

"That depends," he answered tersely.

"I hear you have some *passionately* interesting friends."

"Where did you hear that?"

"Ah, don't you know?" she responded commiser-atingly. "This is the most scandalously gossipy neighbourhood in France. My *dear* young man, every one from here to Timbuctu knows all about it by this time!"

"All about what?"

"About the excitement you're such a *valuable* part of; about your wonderful Spanish friend and how she claims the strange young man here for her husband."

"They'll know more'n that, I expec'," he returned with a side glance at me, "before *very* long."

"Every one thinks *I* am so interesting," she rattled on artlessly, "because I happened to meet *you* in the woods. I've held quite a levee all day.

In a reflected way it makes a heroine of me, you see, because you are one of the very *most* prominent figures in it all. I hope you won't think I've been too bold," she pursued anxiously, "in claiming that I really am one of your acquaintances?"

"That'll be all right," he politely assured her.

"I am so glad." Her laughter rang out gaily. "Because I've been talking about you as if we were the *oldest* friends, and I'd hate to have them find me out. I've told them everything—about your appearance you see, and how your hair was parted, and how you were dressed, and——"

"Luk here," he interrupted, suddenly discharging his Bowery laugh, "did you tell 'em how *he* was dressed?" He pointed a jocular finger at me. "That *wud* 'a' made a hit!"

"No; we weren't talking of him."

"Why not? He's in it, too. Bullieve me, he *thinks* he is!"

"In the excitement, you mean?"

"Right!" said Mr. Percy amiably. "He goes round holdin' Rip Van Winkle Keredec's hand when the ole man's cryin'; helpin' him sneak his trunks off t' Paris—playin' the hired man gener'ly. Oh, he thinks he's quite the boy, in this trouble!"

"I'm afraid it's a small part," she returned, "compared to yours."

"Oh, I hold my end up, I guess."

"I should think you'd be so worn out and sleepy you couldn't hold your head up!"

"Who? *Me?* Not t'-night, m'little friend. I tuk *my* sleep 's aft'noon and let Rameau do the Sherlock a little while."

She gazed upon him with unconcealed admiration. "You are wonderful," she sighed faintly, and *"Wonderful!"* she breathed again. "How prosaic are drawing-lessons," she continued, touching my arm and moving with me toward the pavilion, "after listening to a man of action like that!"

Mr. Percy, establishing himself comfortably in a garden chair at the foot of the gallery steps, was heard to utter a short cough as he renewed the light of his cigarette.

My visitor paused upon my veranda, humming, "Quand l'Amour Meurt" while I went within and lit a lamp. "Shall I bring the light out there?" I asked, but, turning, found that she was already in the room.

"The sketch-book is my duenna," she said, sinking into a chair upon one side of the centre table, upon which I placed the lamp. "Lessons are unquestionable, at any place or time. Behold the beautiful posies!" She spread the book open on the table between us, as I seated myself opposite her, revealing some antique coloured smudges of flowers. "Elegancies of Eighteen-Forty! Isn't that a survival of the period when young ladies had 'accomplishments,' though! I found it at the château and——"

"Never mind," I said. "Don't you know that you can't ramble over the country alone at this time of night?"

"If you speak any louder," she said, with some urgency of manner, "you'll be 'hopelessly compromised socially,' as Mrs. Alderman McGinnis and the Duchess of Gwythyl-Corners say"—she directed my glance, by one of her own, through the open door to Mr. Percy—"because *he'll* hear you and know that the sketch-book was only a shallow pretext of mine to see you. Do be a little manfully self-contained, or you'll get us talked about! And as for 'this time of night,' I believe it's almost half past nine."

"Does Miss Ward know——"

"Do you think it likely? One of the most con-
venient things about a château is the number of
ways to get out of it without being seen. I had a
choice of eight. So I 'suffered fearfully from neu-
ralgia,' dined in my own room, and sped through
the woods to my honest forester." She nodded
brightly. "That's *you!*"

"You weren't afraid to come through the woods
alone?" I asked, uncomfortably conscious that her
gaiety met a dull response from me.

"No."

"But if Miss Ward finds that you're not at the
château——"

"She won't; she thinks I'm asleep. She brought
me up a sleeping-powder herself."

"She thinks you took it?"

"She *knows* I did," said Miss Elliott. "I'm full
of it! And that will be the reason—if you notice
that I'm particularly nervous or excited."

"You seem all of that," I said, looking at her
eyes, which were very wide and very brilliant.
"However, I believe you always do."

"Ah!" she smiled. "I knew you thought me
atrocious from the first. You find *myriads* of
objections to me, don't you?"

I had forgotten to look away from her eyes, and I kept on forgetting. (The same thing had happened several times lately; and each time, by a somewhat painful coincidence, I remembered my age at precisely the instant I remembered to look away.) "Dazzling" is a good old-fashioned word for eyes like hers; at least it might define their effect on me.

"If I did manage to object to you," I said slowly, "it would be a good thing for me—wouldn't it?"

"Oh, I've *won!*" she cried.

"Won?" I echoed.

"Yes. I laid a wager with myself that I'd have a pretty speech from you before I went out of your life"—she checked a laugh, and concluded thrillingly—"forever! I leave Quesnay to-morrow!"

"Your father has returned from America?"

"Oh dear, no," she murmured. "I'll be quite at the world's mercy. I must go up to Paris and retire from public life until he does come. I shall take the vows—in some obscure but respectable *pension.*"

"You can't endure the life at the château any longer?"

"It won't endure *me* any longer. If I shouldn't

go to-morrow I'd be put out, I think—after to-night!"

"But you intimated that no one would know about to-night!"

"The night isn't over yet," she replied enigmatically.

"It almost is—for you," I said; "because in ten minutes I shall take you back to the château gates."

She offered no comment on this prophecy, but gazed at me thoughtfully and seriously for several moments. "I suppose you can imagine," she said, in a tone that threatened to become tremulous, "what sort of an afternoon we've been having up there?"

"Has it been—" I began.

"Oh, heart-breaking! Louise came to my room as soon as they got back from here, this morning, and told me the whole pitiful story. But they didn't let her stay there long, poor woman!"

"They?" I asked.

"Oh, Elizabeth and her brother. They've been at her all afternoon—off and on."

"To do what?"

"To 'save herself,' so they call it. They're insisting that she must not see her poor husband again. They're *determined* she sha'n't."

"But George wouldn't worry her," I objected.

"Oh, wouldn't he?" The girl laughed sadly. "I don't suppose he could help it, he's in such a state himself, but between him and Elizabeth it's hard to see how poor Mrs. Harman lived through the day."

"Well," I said slowly, "I don't see that they're not right. She ought to be kept out of all this as much as possible; and if her husband has to go through a trial——"

"I want you to tell me something," Miss Elliott interrupted. "How much do you like Mr. Ward?"

"He's an old friend. I suppose I like my old friends in about the same way that other people like theirs."

"How much do you like Mr. Saffren—I mean Mr. Harman?"

"Oh, *that!*" I groaned. "If I could still call him 'Oliver Saffren,' if I could still think of him as 'Oliver Saffren,' it would be easy to answer. I never was so 'drawn' to a man in my life before. But when I think of him as Larrabee Harman, I am full of misgivings."

"Louise isn't," she put in eagerly, and with something oddly like the manner of argument. "His wife isn't!"

"Oh, I know. Perhaps one reason is that she never saw him at quite his worst. I did. I had only two glimpses of him—of the briefest—but they inspired me with such a depth of dislike that I can't tell you how painful it was to discover that 'Oliver Saffren'—this strange, pathetic, attractive *friend* of mine—is the same man."

"Oh, but he isn't!" she exclaimed quickly.

"Keredec says he is," I laughed helplessly.

"So does Louise," returned Miss Elliott, disdaining consistency in her eagerness. "And she's right —and she cares more for him than she ever did!"

"I suppose she does."

"Are you—" the girl began, then stopped for a moment, looking at me steadily. "Aren't you a little in love with her?"

"Yes," I answered honestly. "Aren't you?"

"*That's* what I wanted to know!" she said; and as she turned a page in the sketch-book for the benefit of Mr. Percy, I saw that her hand had begun to tremble.

"Why?" I asked, leaning toward her across the table.

"Because, if she were involved in some under-taking—something that, if it went wrong, would endanger her happiness and, I think, even her life—for it might actually kill her if she failed, and brought on a worse catastrophe——"

"Yes?" I said anxiously, as she paused again.

"You'd help her?" she said.

"I would indeed," I assented earnestly. "I told her once I'd do anything in the world for her."

"Even if it involved something that George Ward might never forgive you for?"

"I said, 'anything in the world,'" I returned, perhaps a little huskily. "I meant all of that. If there is anything she wants me to do, I shall do it."

She gave a low cry of triumph, but immediately checked it. Then she leaned far over the table, her face close above the book, and, tracing the outline of an uncertain lily with her small, brown-gloved forefinger, as though she were consulting me on the drawing, "I wasn't afraid to come through the woods alone," she said, in a very low voice, "because I wasn't alone. Louise came with me."

"What?" I gasped. "Where is she?"

"At the Baudry cottage down the road. They

won't miss her at the château until morning; I
locked her door on the outside, and if they go to
bother her again—though I don't think they will—
they'll believe she's fastened it on the inside and is
asleep. She managed to get a note to Keredec late
this afternoon; it explained everything, and he had
some trunks carried out the rear gate of the inn
and carted over to Lisieux to be shipped to Paris
from there. It is to be supposed—or hoped, at
least—that this woman and her people will believe
that means Professor Keredec and Mr. Harman will
try to get to Paris in the same way."

"So," I said, "that's what Percy meant about
the trunks. I didn't understand."

"He's on watch, you see," she continued, turning
a page to another drawing. "He means to sit up
all night, or he wouldn't have slept this afternoon.
He's not precisely the kind to be in the habit of
afternoon naps—Mr. Percy!" She laughed nervously. "That's why it's almost absolutely necessary
for us to have you. If we have—the thing is so
simple that it's certain."

"If you have me for what?" I asked.

"If you'll help"—and, as she looked up, her
eyes, now very close to mine, were dazzling indeed

—"I'll adore you for ever and ever! Oh, *much* longer than you'd like me to!"

"You mean she's going to——"

"I mean that she's going to run away with him again," she whispered.

CHAPTER XXII

AT midnight there was no mistaking the palpable uneasiness with which Mr. Percy, faithful sentry, regarded the behaviour of Miss Elliott and myself as we sat conversing upon the veranda of the pavilion. It was not fear for the security of his prisoner which troubled him, but the unseemliness of the young woman's persistence in remaining to this hour under an espionage no more matronly than that of a sketch-book abandoned on the table when we had come out to the open. The youth had veiled his splendours with more splendour: a long overcoat of so glorious a plaid it paled the planets above us; and he wandered restlessly about the garden in this refulgence, glancing at us now and then with what, in spite of the insufficient revelation of the starlight, we both recognised as a chilling disapproval. The lights of the inn were all out; the courtyard was dark. The Spanish woman and Monsieur Rameau had made their appearance for a moment, half an hour earlier, to exchange a word with their fellow vigilant, and, soon after, the extinguishing of the lamps in their respective apartments denoted their retirement for the night. In the "Grande Suite" all had been dark and silent for an hour. About the whole place the only sign of life, aside from those signs furnished by our three selves, was a rhythmical sound from an open window near the kitchen, where incontrovertibly slumbered our *maître d'hôtel* after the cares of the day.

Upon the occasion of our forest meeting Mr. Percy had signified his desire to hear some talk of Art. I think he had his fill to-night—and more; for that was the subject chosen by my dashing companion, and vivaciously exploited until our awaited hour was at hand. Heaven knows what nonsense I prattled, I do not; I do not think I knew at the time. I talked mechanically, trying hard not to betray my increasing excitement.

Under cover of this traduction of the Muse I served, I kept going over and over the details of Louise Harman's plan, as the girl beside me had outlined it, bending above the smudgy sketch-book. "To make them think the flight is for Paris," she had urged, "to Paris by way of Lisieux. To make that man yonder believe that it is toward Lisieux, while they turn at the crossroads, and drive across the country to Trouville for the morning boat to Havre."

It was simple; that was its great virtue. If they were well started, they were safe; and well started meant only that Larrabee Harman should leave the inn without an alarm, for an alarm sounded too soon meant "racing and chasing on Canoby Lea," before they could get out of the immediate neighbourhood. But with two hours' start, and the pursuit spending most of its energy in the wrong direction—that is, toward Lisieux and Paris—they would be on the deck of the French-Canadian liner to-morrow noon, sailing out of the harbour of Le Havre, with nothing but the Atlantic Ocean between them and the St. Lawrence.

I thought of the woman who dared this flight for her lover, of the woman who came full-armed between him and the world, a Valkyr winging down to bear him away to a heaven she would make for him herself. Gentle as she was, there must have been a Valkyr in her somewhere, or she could not attempt this. She swept in, not only between him and the world, but between him and the destroying demons his own sins had raised to beset him. There, I thought, was a whole love; or there she was not only wife but mother to him.

And I remembered the dream of her I had before I ever saw her, on that first night after I came down to Normandy, when Amédée's talk of "Madame d'Armand" had brought her into my thoughts. I remembered that I had dreamed of finding her statue, but it was veiled and I could not uncover it. And to-night it seemed to me that the veil had lifted, and the statue was a figure of Mercy in the beautiful likeness of Louise Harman. Then Keredec was wrong, optimist as he was, since a will such as hers could save him she loved, even from his own acts.

"And when you come to Monticelli's first style—" Miss Elliott's voice rose a little, and I caught the sound of a new thrill vibrating in it—"you find a hundred others of his epoch doing it quite as well, not a *bit* of a bit less commonplace——"

She broke off suddenly, and looking up, as I had fifty times in the last twenty minutes, I saw that a light shone from Keredec's window.

"I dare say they *are* commonplace," I remarked,

rising. "But now, if you will permit me, I'll offer you my escort back to Quesnay."

I went into my room, put on my cap, lit a lantern, and returned with it to the veranda. "If you are ready?" I said.

"Oh, quite," she answered, and we crossed the garden as far as the steps.

Mr. Percy signified his approval.

"Gunna see the little lady home, are you?" he said graciously. "I was *thinkin'* it was about time, m'self!"

The salon door of the "Grand Suite" opened, above me, and at the sound, the youth started, springing back to see what it portended, but I ran quickly up the steps. Keredec stood in the doorway, bare-headed and in his shirt-sleeves; in one hand he held a travelling-bag, which he immediately gave me, setting his other for a second upon my shoulder.

"Thank you, my good, good friend," he said with an emotion in his big voice which made me glad of what I was doing. He went back into the room, closing the door, and I descended the steps as rapidly as I had run up them. Without pausing, I started for the rear of the courtyard, Miss Elliott accompanying me.

The sentry had watched these proceedings open-mouthed, more mystified than alarmed. "Luk here," he said, "I want t' know whut this means."

"Anything you choose to think it means," I laughed, beginning to walk a little more rapidly. He glanced up at the windows of the "Grande Suite," which were again dark, and began to follow us slowly. "What you gut in that grip?" he asked.

"You don't think we're carrying off Mr. Harman?"

"I reckon *he's* in his room all right," said the youth grimly; "unless he's *flew* out. But I want t' know what you think y're doin'?"

"Just now," I replied, "I'm opening this door."

This was a fact he could not question. We emerged at the foot of a lane behind the inn; it was long and narrow, bordered by stone walls, and at the other end debouched upon a road which passed the rear of the Baudry cottage.

Miss Elliott took my arm, and we entered the lane.

Mr. Percy paused undecidedly. "I want t' know whut you think y're doin'?" he repeated angrily, calling after us.

"It's very simple," I called in turn. "Can't I do an errand for a friend? Can't I even carry his travelling-bag for him, without going into explanations to everybody I happen to meet? And," I added, permitting some anxiety to be marked in my voice, "I think you may as well go back. We're not going far enough to need a guard."

Mr. Percy allowed an oath to escape him, and we heard him muttering to himself. Then his footsteps sounded behind us.

"He's coming!" Miss Elliott whispered, with nervous exultation, looking over her shoulder. "He's going to follow."

"He was sure to," said I.

We trudged briskly on, followed at some fifty paces by the perturbed watchman. Presently I heard my companion utter a sigh so profound that it was a whispered moan.

"What is it?" I murmured.

"Oh, it's the thought of Quesnay and to-morrow; facing them with *this!*" she quavered. "Louise has written a letter for me to give them, but I'll have to tell them——"

"Not alone," I whispered. "I'll be there when you come down from your room in the morning."

We were embarked upon a singular adventure, not unattended by a certain danger; we were tingling with a hundred apprehensions, occupied with the vital necessity of drawing the little spy after us— and that was a strange moment for a man (and an elderly painter-man of no mark, at that!) to hear himself called what I was called then, in a tremulous whisper close to my ear. Of course she has denied it since; nevertheless, she said it—twice, for I pretended not to hear her the first time. I made no answer, for something in the word she called me, and in her seeming to mean it, made me choke up so that I could not even whisper; but I made up my mind that, after *that*, if this girl saw Mr. Earl Percy on his way back to the inn before she wished him to go, it would be because he had killed me.

We were near the end of the lane when the neigh of a horse sounded sonorously from the road beyond.

Mr. Percy came running up swiftly and darted by us.

"Who's that?" he called loudly. "Who's that in the cart yonder?"

I set my lantern on the ground close to the wall, and at the same moment a horse and cart drew up on the road at the end of the lane, showing against the starlight. It was Père Baudry's best horse, a stout gray, that would easily enough make Trouville by daylight. A woman's figure and a man's (the latter that of Père Baudry himself) could be made out dimly on the seat of the cart.

"Who is it, I say?" shouted our excited friend. "What kind of a game d'ye think y're puttin' up on me here?"

He set his hand on the side of the cart and sprang upon the hub of the wheel. A glance at the occupants satisfied him.

"Mrs. Harman!" he yelled. "Mrs. Harman!" He leaped down into the road. "I knowed I was a fool to come away without wakin' up Rameau. But you haven't beat us yet!"

He drove back into the lane, but just inside its entrance I met him.

"Where are you going?" I asked.

"Back to the pigeon-house in a hurry. There's devilment here, and I want Rameau. Git out o' my way!"

"You're not going back," said I.

"The hell I ain't!" said Mr. Percy. "I give

ye two seconds t' git out o' my—*Take yer hands offa me!*"

I made sure of my grip, not upon the refulgent overcoat, for I feared he might slip out of that, but upon the collars of his coat and waistcoat, which I clenched together in my right hand. I knew that he was quick, and I suspected that he was "scientific," but I did it before he had finished talking, and so made fast, with my mind and heart and soul set upon sticking to him.

My suspicions as to his "science" were perfervidly justified. "You long-legged devil!" he yelled, and I instantly received a series of concussions upon the face and head which put me in supreme doubt of my surroundings, for I seemed to have plunged, eyes foremost, into the Milky Way. But I had my left arm around his neck, which probably saved me from a *coup de grâce*, as he was forced to pommel me at half-length. Pommel it was; to use so gentle a word for what to me was crash, bang, smash, battle, murder, earthquake and tornado. I was conscious of some one screaming, and it seemed a consoling part of my delirium that the cheek of Miss Anne Elliott should be jammed tight against mine through one phase of the explosion. My

arms were wrenched, my fingers twisted and tortured, and, when it was all too clear to me that I
could not possibly bear one added iota of physical
pain, the ingenious fiend began to kick my shins
and knees with feet like crowbars.

Conflict of any sort was never my vocation. I
had not been an accessory-during-the-fact to a
fight since I passed the truculent age of fourteen;
and it is a marvel that I was able to hang to that
dynamic bundle of trained muscles—which defines
Mr. Earl Percy well enough—for more than ten
seconds. Yet I did hang to him, as Père Baudry
testifies, for a minute and a half, which seems no
inconsiderable lapse of time to a person under-
going such experiences as were then afflicting me.

It appeared to me that we were revolving in
enormous circles in the ether, and I had long since
given my last gasp, when there came a great roaring
wind in my ears and a range of mountains toppled
upon us both; we went to earth beneath it.

"Ha! you must create violence, then?" roared
the avalanche.

And the voice was the voice of Keredec.

Some one pulled me from underneath my struggling antagonist, and, the power of sight in a hazy,

zigzagging fashion coming back to me, I perceived
the figure of Miss Anne Elliott recumbent beside
me, her arms about Mr. Percy's prostrate body.
The extraordinary girl had fastened upon him, too,
though I had not known it, and she had gone to
ground with us; but it is to be said for Mr. Earl
Percy that no blow of his touched her, and she
was not hurt. Even in the final extremities of temper, he had carefully discriminated in my favour.

Mrs. Harman was bending over her, and, as the
girl sprang up lightly, threw her arms about her.
For my part, I rose more slowly, section by section,
wondering why I did not fall apart; lips, nose, and
cheeks bleeding, and I had a fear that I should need
to be led like a blind man, through my eyelids swell-
ing shut. That was something I earnestly desired
should not happen; but whether it did, or did not—
or if the heavens fell!—I meant to walk back to
Quesnay with Anne Elliott that night, and, mangled,
broken, or half-dead, presenting whatever appearance of the prize-ring or the *abattoir* that I might,
I intended to take the same train for Paris on the
morrow that she did.

For our days together were not at an end; nor
was it hers nor my desire that they should be.

It was Oliver Saffren—as I like to think of him —who helped me to my feet and wiped my face with his handkerchief, and when that one was ruined, brought others from his bag and stanched the wounds gladly received, in the service of his wife.

"I will remember—" he said, and his voice broke. "These are the memories which Keredec says make a man good. I pray they will help to redeem me." And for the last time I heard the child in him speaking: "I ought to be redeemed; I must be, don't you think, for her sake?"

"Lose no time!" shouted Keredec. "You must be gone if you will reach that certain town for the five-o'clock train of the morning." This was for the spy's benefit; it indicated Lisieux and the train to Paris. Mr. Percy struggled; the professor knelt over him, pinioning his wrists in one great hand, and holding him easily to earth.

"Ha! my friend—" he addressed his captive— "you shall not have cause to say we do you any harm; there shall be no law, for you are not hurt, and you are not going to be. But here you shall stay quiet for a little while—till I say you can go." As he spoke he bound the other's wrists with a short rope which he took from his pocket, performing the same office immediately afterward for Mr. Percy's ankles.

"I take the count!" was the sole remark of that philosopher. "I can't go up against no herd of elephants."

"And now," said the professor, rising, "good-bye! The sun shall rise gloriously for you tomorrow. Come, it is time."

The two women were crying in each other's arms. "Good-bye!" sobbed Anne Elliott.

Mrs. Harman turned to Keredec. "Good-bye! for a little while."

He kissed her hand. "Dear lady, I shall come within the year."

She came to me, and I took her hand, meaning to kiss it as Keredec had done, but suddenly she was closer and I felt her lips upon my battered cheek. I remember it now.

I wrung her husband's hand, and then he took her in his arms, lifted her to the foot-board of the cart, and sprang up beside her.

"God bless you, and good-bye!" we called.

And their voices came back to us. "God bless *you* and good-bye!"

They were carried into the enveloping night. We stared after them down the road; watching the lantern on the tail-board of the cart diminish; watching it dim and dwindle to a point of gray;— listening until the hoof-beats of the heavy Norman grew fainter than the rustle of the branch that rose above the wall beside us. But it is bad luck to strain eyes and ears to the very last when friends are parting, because that so sharpens the loneliness; and before the cart went quite beyond our ken, two of us set out upon the longest way to Quesnay.

THE END

THE COUNTRY LIFE PRESS
GARDEN CITY, N. Y.